Romeo and Juliet
Gen Z Edition

Chilliam Shakespeare

Books By Bo

ISBN: 979-8-9900166-0-6

First Printing: January, 2024

This is a work of fiction. Names, characters, places, and incidents either are the product of the author's imagination or are used fictitiously, and any resemblance to actual persons, living or dead, businesses, companies, events, or locales is entirely coincidental.

Printed in U.S.A.

DEDICATION

To all the fam who stay up late scrolling through TikTok instead of cracking open a dusty old book - this one's for you.

To the squad who thinks Shakespeare is a type of fancy coffee and Jane Austen is a new influencer - I gotchu.

To the teachers trying to explain "thou" and "thee" to a classroom of peeps who communicate in emojis - your struggle is real.

And finally, to the OGs of literature, those old-school authors who probably never imagined their works would be translated into Gen Z slang - thanks for not rolling in your graves.

This book is for all of you, the dreamers, the meme-creators, the trendsetters. May the classics live on in our LOL's.

Stay Lit

CONTENTS

Act 4: No Chill Zone

Act 5: The Finale

ACKNOWLEDGMENTS

First off, major props to all the OG writers – y'all didn't have WiFi, but somehow managed to create some epic stories. Respect.

Huge shoutout to my English teacher, Lt. Colonel Boese, who first said, "Shakespeare is like ancient tweets." Mind. Blown.

Mad love to my squad, who endured my constant ramblings about this project and still managed to keep their eyes from glazing over. You're the real MVPs.

Props to the coffee shop down the street – for the Wi-Fi and the endless caffeine, W.

Big thanks to the meme lords of the internet for providing endless inspiration and procrastination material. You keep the dream alive.

To all the haters, read this book and get a vibe check. Its 2024 be a stan.

And lastly, to all the Gen Z peeps reading this – Slay.

ROMEO AND JULIET GEN Z EDITION

CHARACTER INTROS

ROMEO: This dude is like the ultimate softboi, you know? Only 16, but he's deep, low-key handsome, and kinda emo with his whole love obsession. He's all about that peaceful lifestyle, not even down for the fam drama with the Capulets. And when he falls for Juliet, it's like, major vibes. He's so into her, he'd yeet himself out of existence for her. Romeo's also a solid bro to Benvolio, Mercutio, and Friar Lawrence.

JULIET: She's 13, a total baddie, but still figuring things out. Starts off pretty naive about love, but then she gets woke real fast when Romeo slides into her life. Juliet's stuck in that high-class life, can't just bounce around like Romeo. But sis has got guts —FRFR. She's all in for Romeo, even when it gets sketchy. Her ride-or-die is the Nurse, even though they have some beef later.

FRIAR LAWRENCE: This guy's like the chill, wise boomer. A friar, but also a low-key alchemist with those herb skills. He's the one who hooks up Romeo and Juliet, thinking it'll chill out the Verona drama. Friar Lawrence is all about balance and big brain plans.

MERCUTIO: Romeo's bestie and a total savage with words. He's got jokes for days and is not here for posers or clout chasers. Mercutio thinks Romeo's love drama is a bit cringe, he's more about that physical love life.

NURSE: Juliet's day one, the lady who's been there since diapers. She's funny but kinda extra, always dropping those boomer comments. The Nurse is down for Juliet's happiness, but doesn't really get the whole ride-or-die vibe.

TYBALT: Juliet's cousin, a real hypebeast who's all about that Capulet clout. Quick to throw hands if he feels disrespected. He's quick to pull out his weapon and is a hater on all Montagues.

CAPULET & LADY CAPULET: Juliet's parents. Capulet's the boss man, big on respect and finding good matches for Juliet. He loves her but doesn't really get her (he's a bit of a boomer). Lady Capulet's all about that married-young life and pushing Juliet towards Paris.

MONTAGUE & LADY MONTAGUE: Romeo's folks. The Montague's mainly stress about Romeo's emotional phases. Lady Montague's heart is so in it, she literally dies of grief. #Dramatic

PARIS: This is the guy that Capulet and Lady Capulet want Juliet to marry. Thinks he's 'Top G' once he gets the green light to marry Juliet.

BENVOLIO: Romeo's cousin, the peacekeeper. He's trying to keep things chill in the streets of Verona, and he's always trying to get Romeo's mind off his toxic love life.

PRINCE ESCALUS: The big boss of Verona. He's related to Mercutio and Paris, and his main goal is to keep the peace in the city, no matter what.

FRIAR JOHN: Another friar, tasked with delivering the news about Juliet's fake death to Romeo. But, the dude gets stuck in quarantine (big yikes), and the message never makes it.

BALTHASAR: Romeo's loyal servant, the one who hits him with the fake news of Juliet's death, not knowing it's just a plot.

SAMPSON and GREGORY: These are Capulet's hype men, always ready to start some drama with the Montagues. While Gregory is a little more grounded, Sampson is always down to do it for the plot.

ABRAHAM: Montague's servant, who gets into it with Sampson and Gregory in the very first throwdown of the play.

The APOTHECARY: A Mantua drug dealer, basically. He's broke, so he throws morals out the window and sells Romeo the poison for a quick bag.

PETER: A Capulet servant, he's the one getting people to the Capulet's party and helps the Nurse link up with Romeo. Dude can't read and definitely won't win "The Voice."

ROSALINE: She's the girl Romeo was obsessing over before Juliet. She's like an IG model – never seen but always talked about.

The CHORUS: This is the narrator, dropping all the tea about the plot and themes, like a Twitter thread keeping everyone updated.

THE PROLOGUE

(CHORUS rolls up on stage)

CHORUS: Hey, fam! We're hitting up the gorgeous town of Verona, where our story's poppin' off. There's this ancient beef between two crews, and things are getting real extra - folks are getting their hands all kinds of dirty. Aight, now check this: Two unlucky kids from these feuding fams catch feels, HARD, and end up becoming actual ride-or-dies.. Yeah, literally. Their wild ride to the afterlife is what finally squashes the two families' beef. For the next couple of hours, we're gonna serve you the story of their cursed romance and the fam drama that only their fatal moment could halt. Grab your popcorn and get comfortable, kings, queens, and everything in between. We're about to pour some piping-hot tea and make up for anything we might've skipped in this hype intro.

(CHORUS dips out)

Act 1: The Hype Begins

Scene 1: Squad Meetup

Setting: A bustling street in the city. It's like the main strip where everyone hangs out, complete with cafes, shops, and that one spot where everyone seems to run into each other.

(Sampson and Gregory, Capulet's squad, roll up strapped, ready to stir up some drama)

SAMPSON: Ayo Gregory, for real, we can't let those Montague clowns play us. We cant let them trash talk us.

GREGORY: Bruh, you're the one always talking a lot of trash. It's giving garbage man.

SAMPSON: Nah, what I'm saying is if they start something, we're gonna finish it. Straps out and all.

GREGORY: You need to chill and try not to get in over your head. That ain't it, chief.

SAMPSON: Trust me, I throw down hard when I'm heated.

GREGORY: Its tough to make you salty though.

SAMPSON: Just seeing one of those Montague dogs can get me worked up.

GREGORY: Worked up enough to dip out with your tail between your legs. You ain't about that life chief.

SAMPSON: Nah, bet. If a Montague gets me pressed, I'll make sure I'm the one walking near the wall and he's the one in the gutter.

GREGORY: That just means you're soft, bro cause betas get pinned up against the wall.

SAMPSON: Nah. The only ones getting pinned up against walls will be the Montague women—they're easy.

GREGORY: The beef is only between our bosses and their crew.

SAMPSON: I don't care, I'm gonna go off on em. After I throw hands with the opps, I'll finesse the ladies.

GREGORY: Psh, take several seats. I cant even with you rn.

(ABRAM and another Montague servant enter)

SAMPSON: Ayo, Whip out your blickie, bruh. These guys roll with the Montagues.

GREGORY *(whips it out)*: I got my 9 out. It's about to be on sight, I got your back. You sure you're not about to dip out on me?

SAMPSON: Don't trip, I got you.

GREGORY: I'm not gonna lie, you got me mad worried rn.

SAMPSON: Bruh, let's not start anything. We'll let them make the first move.

GREGORY: I'll just throw them a dirty look. They can take it however they want.

SAMPSON: Bet, emote on 'em. If they let it slide, they're simps.

(SAMPSON Fortnite emotes).

ABRAM *(seeing SAMPSON)*: Ayo, you emoting bruh?

SAMPSON: Facts! No print.

ABRAM: On god, I know you ain't doing what I'm thinking.

SAMPSON *(to GREGORY whispering)*: We good with the law if I say 'yeah'?

GREGORY *(to SAMPSON whispering)*: Nah, fam.

ABRAM *(noticing)*: You finna start something?

SAMPSON: If you wanna throw hands, I'm your guy. My squad goes off.

ABRAM: Your little crew of NPC's are basic af compared to mine.

SAMPSON: Cringe, you have no steez.

(BENVOLIO pops in)

GREGORY *(whispering to SAMPSON)*: Say @ me. Lowkey, we got backup coming.

SAMPSON *(to ABRAM)*: @ me fool!

ABRAM: You ready for a clapback?

SAMPSON: Aight, draw your strap if you're high-key triggered.

(to Gregory)

Gregory, start blasting!

(And then, they started blasting)

BENVOLIO *(drawing his strap)***:** Break it up, you clowns! Sheathe your gats! Bruh, y'all are so extra.

(TYBALT enters)

TYBALT: Seriously? You're out here scrapping with these nobodies? Turn around, Benvolio, face the dude who's about to put you on blast.

BENVOLIO: Yo, fam, chill with all that. Either stash that glock or use it to help me kill this beef.

TYBALT: For real? How're you gonna pull your out strap, then talk peace? I cant even with all this back and forth. Let's finish what you started!

(BENVOLIO and TYBALT fight. A bunch of CITIZENS rush in, hyped, carrying bats and makeshift weapons)

CITIZENS: Ayo grab those bats! Put these dudes on blast!
Down with the Capulets! Montagues are cancelled! We're tired af of your beef!

(CAPULET rolls up in his Gandalf robe, with LADY CAPULET)

CAPULET: What's all this ruckus? Hand me my glock, I'm gonna clapback rn.

LADY CAPULET: Chill boomer. What you need is a walking stick, not a strap.

(MONTAGUE busts in, strapped up, with LADY MONTAGUE)

MONTAGUE: Hand me my piece. That Capulet loser is here, flexing his gun just to press me.

CAPULET: Old man Montague!

(his wife holds him back)

Back off! Don't hold me back fam!

LADY MONTAGUE: Nah, you ain't stepping nowhere near that fool.

(Enter PRINCE ESCALUS with his crew)

PRINCE ESCALUS: Hey, listen up goblins! They ain't listening, for real? —Ayo, you there! Y'all extra af, gettin' all hype and spillin' each other's blood! High-key, I'll make you regret it if you don't drop those weapons and hear preach right quick.

(MONTAGUE, CAPULET, and their crews ditch their weapons)

On god, this is the third time y'all caused chaos in our streets, all cause YOU, Capulet and Montague, have zero chill. Three times you've killed our vibes, and the citizens of Verona had to grab some dusty spears to break y'all dummies up. If y'all start trippin' in our streets again, no cap I'm cancelling every one of you. Everyone else, go home.

PRINCE ESCALUS *(to CAPULET)*: You, Capulet, roll with me.

(to MONTAGUE)

And Montague, slide through to my courthouse. I'll let you know what's else I need from you. And for the rest of y'all, I'm saying it on loud: dip out or it's GG for you.

(Everyone dips except MONTAGUE, LADY MONTAGUE, and BENVOLIO)

MONTAGUE: Who's the main character that started this? Nephew! You were here when it popped off, right?

BENVOLIO: Woah-woah-woah, Linda, listen. Before I even rolled up, your peeps were already throwin' down with your enemy's crew. So I pulled out my 9 to break 'em up, right? Then, that hot-headed Tybalt crashes in, blickie out, all ready to clap back. Dude was taunting me, swinging his 45. So, then I started blasting. The crowd's getting heated, more heads keep jumping in. Then the Prince rolls in and shuts it all down.

LADY MONTAGUE: Damn. It be like that sometimes. Where's Romeo at? Have you seen him today? Glad he wasn't around for this brawl.

BENVOLIO: So early this morning, way before the sun got up, I was all in my feels, so I went for a stroll. Over by the trees on the west siiide, I spotted your boy Romeo out for a morning walk. I started heading his way, but homie saw me and ghosted into the woods. Probably just wanted to ride solo and get away from all the drama, just like me. I thought, cool, he's dodging me. So I let him be and did my own thing.

MONTAGUE: Dude's been spotted there a lot, being straight up emo, Looking like a MySpace profile picture. But no cap, as soon as the sun peeks out in the east, that little emo kid heads home to dodge the daylight. Man, he's all up in his room, locked away, shutting out the daylight, dark and moody AF. This vibe he's on, it's hella extra.

BENVOLIO: Uncle, you got any idea why he's all like this?

MONTAGUE: I'm clueless. He's been acting real sus and secretive as of late.

BENVOLIO: You sure you've been doing the most to get him to spill the tea?

MONTAGUE: Straight up, I've tried. And so has the crew, but he's left me on read. He's high-key cringe. It's a sad story and hes the main character. If we could just figure out why he's so down, we'd be hella down to help, no cap.

(Enter ROMEO)

BENVOLIO: Speak of the devil, here comes Romeo. Aight, if it's cool with you, I'm gonna pull him to the side. He's gotta spill the tea to me.

MONTAGUE: Alrighty, you go Glen Coco.

(To his wife)

Let's leave them be, Queen.

(Exit MONTAGUE and LADY MONTAGUE)

BENVOLIO: Ayo cuz, morning.

ROMEO: Is it really that early?

BENVOLIO: Yeah, it's just hit nine. On god.

ROMEO: Fr, time drags when you're feeling low. Was that my pops who just dipped?

BENVOLIO: Yup, that was him. What's got you so down, you look like you're in a Nickelback music video. Huge L.

ROMEO: I'm lowkey simping fam.

BENVOLIO: You caught feels, huh?

ROMEO: More like, feels caught me and I'm tapped out.

BENVOLIO: You out of love to give?

ROMEO: Nah, I'm into someone. The problem is, she isn't feeling me back.

BENVOLIO: That's tough king. You sound down bad.

ROMEO: Facts, its wild how loves supposed to be blind but it can still leave you on read.

(*noticing blood on the streets*)

Whoa! What's all this mess? Nah actually, don't even say it—I already know the deal. This beef is more about love than hate. Oh, brawling love, loving hate! Love that's straight up nothing! Sad-happy vibes! Serious jokes! Love's heavy and light, bright and dark, hot and cold, sick and healthy, both sleep and wake—it is what it is.

BENVOLIO: Buh, you're acting like the main character with long monologues like that. But yeah fam.. I feel for you right now.

ROMEO: For real? Over what?

BENVOLIO: Being a simp is so cringe I feel bad for you.

ROMEO: That's just how love does you dirty. Love is like following someone and then waiting anxiously for them to follow you back. What else is it? It's low-key madness, feels like an L but somehow still a banger. Falling in love with someone is even more frightening. It's like handing someone a gun and hoping they never pull the trigger on you. Anyway, I'm out.

BENVOLIO: Bruh, again, chill with the rants. Are you bailing on me now? That's cold.

ROMEO: I gotta dip. I feel like I lost myself. This ain't Romeo; he's somewhere else.

BENVOLIO: Just spill the tea man. Who are you all messed up over?

ROMEO: What, you want me to sob and tell you?

BENVOLIO: No need to sob, bro. Just spill the tea loser. Who is it?

ROMEO: Telling a dying man to write his will is just gonna make him die quicker. No cap, Benvolio, I'm all about this girl.

BENVOLIO: Bruh, you're the down bad CEO.

ROMEO: Damn, Facts.

BENVOLIO: The hotter the target, the quicker it's hit.

ROMEO: Nah, you missed the mark. She won't let Cupid's arrow touch her. She's high-key a nun. She's immune to love's weak game. Won't open DM slides, won't catch feels. She's a total VSCO girl but her looks will die with her.

BENVOLIO: She's gonna stay single forever?

ROMEO: Yep, she's living that nun life. It's big yikes, bro. No mini-me's means her genes won't live on. She's too boujee and brainy, but it's like I'm cursed. No romance, and here I am, half alive, simping over her.

BENVOLIO: Bro, you gotta get your head straight.

ROMEO: Then teach me how to forget she exists!

BENVOLIO: Yo, Romeo, just let your eyes wander, fam. Scope out some other women.

ROMEO: Bro, that's just gonna make me simp harder for her glow up. You know how these queens rock those sleek black masks? Those masks just got me thinking 'bout how fire they are underneath. It's like, once you've seen something epic, you can't unsee it, you feel me? Tell me about a fire chick, and all I think about is she's just a DM slide from someone better than me. I'm out, bro. You can't help someone this down bad.

BENVOLIO: Romeo, say less. I'll show you how to swipe left on that heartache fam.

(They exit, Benvolio checking his phone, Romeo lost in thought)

Act 1

Scene 2: DM's and Plans

Setting: *A street. Just a typical street in Verona, where plans get cooked up and schemes are set.*

CAPULET *(continuing a conversation)*: But Montague's on the same no-beef oath as me, and he's facing the same penalties. Keeping it chill shouldn't be so hard for OGs like us.

PARIS: Both of you have mad respect, it's sus that you've been at it for so long. But also, what's the word on my request?

CAPULET: I'm just gonna keep it 100. my girl's still little a baby, hasn't even hit 14. Let's cool it for like two more summers before we start thinking of wedding hashtags.

PARIS: There's plenty of girls younger than her already rocking the mom life and loving it.

CAPULET: Those young brides be growing up way too fast. But aight, shoot your shot, Paris. Slide into her DMs. My word's only part of the deal. If she's down to put a ring on it, my blessing will seal the deal. Tonight, we're throwing this epic banger we do every year. Got my squad coming through, and I'mma add you to the VIP list. My crib's gonna be lit tonight, with stars walking around like they own the place, lighting up the scene from the ground up. The ladies there will be fresh as the new Yeezy drops. Check out anyone, pick that passes the vibe check. Once you see the lineup, my daughter might not seem like the mood anymore. Let's bounce.

(to PETER, handing him a paper)

Little man, take a lap around Verona. Hit up the folks on this list and tell 'em they're VIPs at my pad tonight.

(CAPULET and PARIS exit)

PETER *(looking at the list)*: Find these names? That's like saying sneakerheads should mess with hoodies, and Andriod users should use iMessage. Damn, I gotta track these peeps down, and I can't read! Huge   L.

(Sees ROMEO AND BENVOLIO)

Oh, talk about perfect timing, here come some dudes.

(BENVOLIO and ROMEO enter.)

BENVOLIO *(to ROMEO)*: Romeo, you can kill one heartache by sparking a new one. A fresh baddie can make the old pain fade. It's like stopping the spins by turning the other way. Get your mind on a new girl, and your old crush will feel like old news.

ROMEO: Yo, the plantain leaf is high-key magic for that.

BENVOLIO *(looking at him like he's crazy)*: The plantain leaf? For what, dude?

ROMEO: For when you eat it on an L day.

BENVOLIO: What? Romeo, you buggin?

ROMEO: Nah, man, I'm just trapped tighter than a phone without service. I'm like locked in a room with no Wi-Fi, starving for likes. I'm getting ghosted and left on read…   .

(to PETER)

What's up, my guy?

PETER: Hey fam. Do you how to read?

ROMEO: Only thing I'm reading is my own sus love life.

PETER *(assuming Romeo doesn't know his letters)*: Low key depressing af, but it sounds like you learned that from life, not books. But for real, can you read anything you see?

ROMEO: Yeah, if it's in my DMs and I know the emojis.

PETER: Pluh. You are not passing the vibe check. Have a good one… wierdo.

ROMEO: Hold up, I can read. On god.

(he reads the letter)

"Signor Martino and his squad,
Count Anselme and his Insta-famous sisters,
The widow Vitruvio,
Signor Placentio and his two nieces,
Mercutio and his bro Valentine,
Uncle Capulet and his fam,
My cousin Rosaline and Livia,
Signor Valentio and his cuz Tybalt,
Lucio and the hypebeast Helena."

Dang, that's a lit guest list. Where they pulling up?

PETER: To our crib.

ROMEO: To grub?

PETER: Yeah, to our pad.

ROMEO: Whose pad?

PETER: My boss's place.

ROMEO: For real, I should've asked who your boss was from the jump.

PETER: Imma tell you so you don't have to ask. My boss is the Top G, Capulet. If you ain't rolling with the Montague crew, you can slide through.

(PETER strolls out)

BENVOLIO: Ayo! Your crush Rosaline's gonna be at Capulet's kickback, along with all the baddies of Verona. Slide thru and scope out some other baddies. The girl you're gassing up is gonna look mid.

ROMEO: If my eyes ever play me like that, may my tears burn them from the inside! A baddie more stunning than my girl? Bruh, even the sun hasn't seen anyone that fire since day one of the 'gram.

BENVOLIO: Look, bro, you started hyping her up when there was no competition. It was just her in your feed, no one else to compare. But let your eyes peep her side-by-side with another baddie at this kickback, and you won't be all in your feels about her being such a snack.

ROMEO: Aight, I'll roll with you. Not cause I think you're gonna put me on to someone better, but just so I can catch a glimpse of the girl who's got my heart feeling extra.

(They bounce, heading towards the Capulet's party)

Act 1

Scene 3: Family Tea & Drama

Setting: *The squad's hangout at the Capulet House, a cozy room in the house where the squad gathers to spill tea and plot their next moves. There's that one comfy couch everyone fights over.*

(LADY CAPULET and the NURSE roll in)

LADY CAPULET: Nurse, where's my daughter? Tell her to come through.

NURSE: I already hit her up. Juliet! Where you at queen?

(Juliet pops in)

JULIET: What's good fam? Who's calling?

NURSE: Your mom's looking for you.

20

JULIET: Hey, Mom. What's the tea?

LADY CAPULET: Nurse, can you give us some space? We gotta have the real talk—wait, actually, Nurse, stay. You know Juliet's whole story.

NURSE: Facts.

LADY CAPULET: She's not even fourteen.

NURSE: I'd bet my follower count on it—but real talk, I've only got like four followers—she's not fourteen yet. How long till Lammastide?

LADY CAPULET: Two weeks and some change.

NURSE: Aigh lemme spill some tea 'bout Juliet. Homegirl's about to hit fourteen on Lammas Eve, legit. Feels like just yesterday, she was a tiny bae along with her bud Susan—RIP, girl. Anyway, Susan's chilling in heaven, but Jules is gonna level up to fourteen. Facts, no printer. So, check it, it's been a whole decade plus one since that cray-cray earthquake shook things up. Juliet was just a lil' munchkin then, straight up stopped breastfeeding that day. No cap, I remember 'cause I had this bitter AF wormwood on me, chilling under the sun, by the dove house. You guys were out in Mantua, living your best life. But yo, when Juliet got a taste of that bitter game on my boob, she was not having it. Started beefing with my chest, no joke. Then bam! Earthquake city. I was like, "I'm out," didn't need anyone telling me twice. That's eleven years back. Jules was already on her feet, running and tripping all cute-like. Oh, and get this—she had this little oopsie on her forehead just a day before. My man, bless his soul, picked her up and was all like, "Yo, Jule, did you faceplant? Bet you'll be falling back when you get woke." And I'm dead, 'cause she just stops crying, looks up, and is like, "Yeah." Dude, that moment was straight-up iconic. "You'll fall back, Jule," he said, and she's like, "Yeah, bet." Lowkey wish I could relive that LOL. Like, imagine if I'm around for a millennium, that's the story I'm telling everyone. "Won't you, Jule," he said, and she was like, "Yeah, I gotchu."

LADY CAPULET: Alright alright, chill with the stories. You're a huge stan we get it.

NURSE: I just gotta say, it's straight-up hilarious every time I think 'bout Jules cutting the waterworks to drop a "Facts." No joke, she had this forehead bruise the size of a chunky avocado toast—legit painful. She was bawling her eyes out, and then my dude comes in with the banter, all "Yo, Jule, you faceplanted, huh? Bet you'll be dropping sick moves at the club when you're older, right?" And she just kills the tears and hits us with a "Facts." Like, how adorbs is that?

JULIET: Okay, Nurse, that's enough.

NURSE: Aight, I'm done. God bless you with all the hearts and likes. You were the cutest baby ever. If I see you get wifed up, my life's goals are complete.

LADY CAPULET: Speaking of getting wifed up, that's what we need to talk about. Juliet, what you think about marriage?

JULIET: Marriage? That's like a blue check I never thought I'd get.

LADY CAPULET: : You gotta start thinking about it, though. In Verona, girls younger than you, real influencers, are already moms. By your age, I was already your mom, and you're still living that single life. So here's the scoop: Paris is super into you.

NURSE: What a catch, Juliet. Dude's on top of the game, like he's straight out of a Vogue cover.

LADY CAPULET: Totally. He's like Harry Styles, but post-One Direction.

NURSE: Facts! No print.

LADY CAPULET *(to Juliet)*: So, what's your take? Can you vibe with this dude? Tonight, you'll peep him at our party. Check out Paris's profile and get lost in his hotness. Scope out his features, see how they come together to make him a total snack. If you're still on the fence, just get lost in his eyes. Dude's single, only missing a queen to make him insta-perfect. I mean, fish belong in the sea, right? And a baddie like you shouldn't be hiding from a hottie like him. Everyone's saying he's eye candy, and being his girl, you'd be just as IG-worthy. You'd get to share his clout, and by choosing him, you ain't losing a thing.

NURSE: Losing nothing? Girl, you'd be gaining, for real. Dudes tend to add a few pounds, you know, with the baby and all.

LADY CAPULET *(to Juliet)*: So, what's the word? You down to slide in his DM's?

JULIET: I'll scope him out and try to catch feels, at least if there's something to double-tap. But I won't let myself go all heart-eyes more than you say I can.

(PETER enters.)

PETER: Ayo, madam, the squad's all here. Dinner's ready, peeps are asking for you, they're hitting up Juliet, and in the kitchen, they're throwing shade at the Nurse. It's all kinds of wild. I gotta bounce and play host. Slide through when you can.

LADY CAPULET: Bet, we're right behind you. Juliet, Paris is waiting, all eyes on you.

NURSE: Wheels up queen, find yourself a dude who's gonna make your days lit and your nights even littier.

(Narrator shakes in disapproval of that line, They all exit, heading towards the party.)

Act 1

Scene 4: Pregame & Fits

Setting: *Back to the streets, Another slice of Verona's streets where the night's plans get hyped up.*

ROMEO: Yo, what's our story for crashing this gig? We just gonna yeet ourselves in there, no apologies?

BENVOLIO: Bruh, nobody does long intros anymore. We're not about to come in all extra with some Cupid cosplay, scaring off the ladies.

MERCUTIO: Facts, no rehearsed lines, my guy. Keep it lowkey. We slide in, hit them with our sick moves, then ghost.

ROMEO: Hand me a torch, fam. Dancing's not my vibe tonight. Got the sads, big yikes.

MERCUTIO: C'mon, Romeo, don't be a simp. Join the hype.

ROMEO: Nah, fam, I'm out. You've got the drip for dancing. I'm like a boomer with these heavy feels, can't even get lit.

MERCUTIO: Bro, you're the love GOAT! Throw on some Cupid wings, and let's get this bread.

ROMEO: Nah, Cupid's got me all twisted, bro. His arrow's got me shook. This heavy heart's got me grounded.

MERCUTIO: Dude, if you're down bad, you're just dragging love down with you. Don't be sus with love, bro.

ROMEO: Is love even chill? Feels more like it's savage, throwing shade, wild, like a major oof..

MERCUTIO: If love's throwing shade, you gotta clapback. Flex on love and win on your own terms. Yo, pass me a mask. Mask for my mask, you know? Who cares if someone clocks my flaws? Let my mask take the L.

(they put on masks)

BENVOLIO: Squad goals: as soon as we're in, we show our moves.

ROMEO: I'm sticking with the torch. The light-hearted can flex. Old saying: You can't lose if you don't play. I'm just gonna chill and scope out the scene. Looks lit, but I'm on the bench.

MERCUTIO: Bro, you're being a major buzzkill. Don't be all paranoid like a cop on a stakeout. If you're stuck, we'll pull you out—no shade, just saying—where you're deep in your feels. Let's bounce, time's ticking.

ROMEO: Nah, we're chill. It's night, bro.

MERCUTIO: I mean, we're burning through torchlight, wasting it like it's daylight. Use your big brain, not just your basic senses.

ROMEO: Our intentions are valid for hitting up this masquerade, but it feels kinda sus.

MERCUTIO: Why's that?

ROMEO: I had this wild dream last night.

MERCUTIO: Same here, bro.

ROMEO: So what did your dream say?

MERCUTIO: Told me dreamers talk a lot of cap.

ROMEO: They chat nonsense in bed while dreaming up some real stuff.

MERCUTIO: Oh, looks like you ran into Queen Mab then.

ROMEO: Queen who?

MERCUTIO: Mab, she's like the OG fairy squad leader of dreams, for real. She's tiny, like the diamond on a hypebeast's icy chain. She's got this micro ride, pulled by atom-sized horses, straight cruising over bros' noses while they're out like a light. Her whip? Spider legs, legit. Her roof? Made of grasshopper wings, no cap. The reins? We're talking the finest spider web silk. The bar? All moonbeam stuff. Her whip? Just a cricket bone on a thread. And her chauffeur? A tiny gray bug, tinier than the lazy worm from a couch potato's finger. Her chariot? It's this nutty little hazelnut shell, probably whipped up by some OG squirrel or an old-timey grub. Those little guys have been in the fairy Uber business since way back. Queen Mab's out here zipping through lover's brains, sparking all those romantic dreams. She skrrts over courtiers' knees, and they're dreaming of getting low. Slides across lawyers' fingers, and bam, they're dreaming of making bank. Glides over ladies' lips, and they're all about those dreamy kisses. But yo, sometimes she leaves them with blisters 'cause they're

26

breathing all sweet and stuff. She'll cruise into a courtier's mouth, and he's dreaming of flexing with riches. Tickles a priest's nose, and he's dreaming of fat stacks in donations. Rolls over a soldier's neck, and he's dreaming of epic battles, sneaky ambushes, slicing up with Spanish swords, and wild ragers. Then she bangs a drum in his ear, and dude wakes up, shook.

ROMEO: ...Chill fam. Mercutio, you gotta stop. You're spitting straight nonsense.

MERCUTIO: True, true. Dreams are just the brain on autopilot, all air, no substance.

BENVOLIO: This wind you're on about's got us drifting off track. Dinners wrapped up, and we're gonna roll up late.

ROMEO: Lowkey worried we're too early. Got this feeling that tonight's gonna be sus af, ending in my own downfall. But let's get this bread for the plot. Let's get it, simp squad!

BENVOLIO: LFG!

(They march around the stage, drumming up the hype, and exit towards the Capulet's party)

Act 1

Scene 5: This Party's Lit

Setting: *A grand ballroom turned party central. Think pulsing music, mood lighting, and everyone trying to look their best.*

(after a sick dinner party. The vibes are up. PETER and other SERVINGMEN, vibing with napkins, are getting things sorted)

PETER: Yo, where's the diswasher hiding? Dude's MIA on dish duty. He should be grinding those plates clean, not ghosting!

FIRST SERVINGMAN: For real, when only a few homies know the drill and even they're playing lazy, it's a straight-up circus.

PETER: Aight, shift those chairs, wipe down the counters, stash those dishes. And snag me some of that sweet marzipan. Broski, slide a word to the doorkeeper to let in Susan Grindstone and Nell. Where you at, Antony, Potpan?

SECOND SERVINGMAN: On it, chief.

PETER: They're yapping for you in the main hall.

FIRST SERVINGMAN: Bruh, I can't be in two places at once, can I?

(Enter CAPULET with COUSIN, TYBALT, LADY CAPULET, JULIET, and other fam. They bump into ROMEO, BENVOLIO, MERCUTIO, and other guests and PARTYGOERS)

CAPULET: Welcome, fam! Ladies who aren't tripping over their own feet get ready to throw down. Aye, my girls, who's gonna play hard to get now? Bet the shy ones are faking sore feet. Haha, gotcha! Welcome again, fellas. Back in my prime, I could rock a mask and charm a lady or two. Aight, DJs, drop those beats!

(Music slaps and everyone's grooving. ROMEO is on the sidelines)

Make some room, people! Show your moves, ladies!

(to SERVINGMEN)

Get this place glowing, slackers! Clear the floor, flip those tables. And someone turn down the heat – it's too hot in here.

(to his COUSIN)

Bro, this party's lit, right? Nah, chill, chill, my good Capulet cuz. You and I? We're past our prime for these dance floor shenanigans.

(CAPULET and his COUSIN park it)

When was the last time we masked up for a shindig like this?

CAPULET'S COUSIN: Dude, it's been a minute. Like, thirty years?

CAPULET: What? Nah, man, you trippin'. It ain't been that long. Since Lucentio's wedding, for real. Time flies, but it's just been a quarter century since we were incognito.

CAPULET'S COUSIN: For real, it's been longer. Lucentio's kid's over thirty now, chief.

CAPULET: You playin' with me? His son was just a young gun two years ago.

ROMEO (*to a SERVINGMAN, pointing at a girl*)**:** Yo, who's that baddie with the knight over there?

SERVINGMAN: No clue, boss.

ROMEO: Bruh, she's outshining these torches! She's like ice against the night, a gem shining in the dark. She's too bussin' for this world; her vibe's on another level.

TYBALT (*Recognizing ROMEO's voice*)**:** That voice... gotta be a Montague.

(to his PAGE)

Yo, fetch my piece, kid. What's this clown doing at our party, all masked up, trying to clown us? On my fam's honor, it'd be no foul to drop him.

CAPULET (*interrupting*)**:** Yo, Tybalt, my guy, why you buggin'?

TYBALT: Unc, that's a Montague – our rival. That fool Romeo's here just to troll our party.

CAPULET: Romeo, that kid?

TYBALT: Yeah, that clown, Romeo.

CAPULET: Chill, nephew. Let the kid chill. Dude's got a solid rep in Verona, a legit guy. Wouldn't diss him in my own house for all the clout in the world. So cool it, play it smooth. Ignore him. That's what I'm saying. If you respect me, you'll chill and put on a happy face. No beefing at my party.

TYBALT: Nah, Uncle. I can't deal with this dude here. It ain't right.

CAPULET: ou will stand it, young blood. You heard me. I'm running this show, right? You won't start no drama at my bash. No way!

TYBALT: But, Unc, it's mad disrespect.

CAPULET: Nah, you're the one out of pocket, kid. Acting all childish. You tryna step to me? Aight, I'll put you in your place.

(to the GUESTS)

Aight, party people, keep vibing!

(to TYBALT)

You're being a punk, back off. Zip it, or else...

(to SERVINGMEN)

Yo, we need more light up in here!

(to the GUESTS)

Everyone, keep having a blast!

(The beats drop again, and the party's back in full swing)

TYBALT *(seething with anger):* This is whack. Holding back is wrecking me. I'm out for now, but Romeo's little stunt, all sweet now, is gonna taste sour real soon.

(TYBALT bounces out, heated.)

(The scene shifts to a early era Taylor Swift vibe as ROMEO and JULIET finally connect)

(ROMEO, all smooth, steps up to JULIET.)

ROMEO *(Grasping JULIET's hand)*: Yo, your hand is like a sacred spot that my hand's not cool enough to chill at. If you're buggin' about my touch, my lips are right here, ready to make it all good with a kiss.

JULIET: Chill, pilgrim, you're too hard on yourself. By holding my hand, you're just showing respect. I mean, pilgrims hold hands with saint statues, right? Palm to palm is like a low-key kiss.

ROMEO: But don't saints and pilgrims got lips too?

JULIET: Yeah, pilgrim, they got lips for praying, though.

ROMEO: Aight, then, saint, let lips do what hands do. I'm praying for a kiss here. Hook me up, so I don't lose hope.

JULIET: Saints stay still, even when they're answering prayers.

ROMEO: Then stay put while I show my devotion.

(He kisses her)

ROMEO: Now your lips have lifted my sin.

JULIET: So, do my lips hold your sin now?

ROMEO: Your sweetness makes sinning tempting. Pass that sin back.

(They kiss again, hella Love Story vibes)

JULIET: You got mad kissing skills, like you've been studying.

NURSE *(interrupting)*: Yo, Juliet! Your mom's looking for you.

(JULIET moves away)

ROMEO (to NURSE): Who's her mom, though?

NURSE: That lady? She's the queen vof this crib, mad respectable. I raised her daughter, the one you've been chatting up. Heads up, the guy who bags her will be rolling in guap.

ROMEO (to himself): She's a Capulet? Dang, that's a tough break. I'm vibing with the enemy.

BENVOLIO *(to ROMEO):* Yo, Romeo, let's dip. Best to bounce when the party's at its peak.

ROMEO: True, but now I'm in deeper than before.

CAPULET *(To the guests):* Hold up, fam, don't jet just yet. We got desserts on the way. *(They whisper to him)* For real? Much love, much love. Good looking out, homies. Aight, good night. Light this place up! Let's hit the hay.

(to his COUSIN)

Bruh, it's late. I'm about to crash.

(Everyone but JULIET and NURSE starts to head out.)

The party's over, but the drama's just beginning for JULIET.

JULIET (Nudging the NURSE): Ayo, Nurse. Who's that dude?

NURSE: That's the son and heir of old Tiberio.

JULIET: And the one dipping out right now?

NURSE: Oh, him? That's young Petruchio, I think.

JULIET: What about the one trailing, the one who didn't dance?

NURSE: No idea who he is.

JULIET (Rushing): Find out, ASAP rocky!

(NURSE dips quick)

If he's hitched, I'ma be crushed – rather die than marry someone else.

(NURSE comes back)

NURSE: His name's Romeo, a Montague. The only son of your fam's archenemy.

JULIET (To herself): Dang, the only guy I'm vibing with is the son of the only dude I despise! I saw him too soon without knowing him, and now I find out too late! Love's wild, making me fall for my number one hater.

NURSE: What are you mumbling about?

JULIET: Just a line I picked up from some guy I danced with.

(Someone yells "Juliet!" offstage)

JULIET: Coming, coming! Let's roll, Nurse. All the guests bounced.

(They exit, closing the scene)

Act 2: Feels and Reels

Prologue

(The CHORUS steps up again to set the scene for the new act.)

CHORUS: Check it, now Romeo's old crush is out the window, and he's all about that new flame. He was all "cause tonight will be the night I will fall for yew" over Rosaline, ready to drop dead for her. But next to Juliet? Rosaline's got nothing. Now, it's like a mutual Insta-like – both Romeo and Juliet are double-tapping on each other's pics. But peep this – Romeo's gotta slide into the DM's of a girl who's basically his enemy. And Juliet? She's caught feels for someone she's supposed to steer clear of. Romeo can't can't chat her up like any regular dude in love. Juliet's in the same boat, crushing hard but can't even hit him up. Yet love's got them feeling like superheroes, and time's about to give them a shot. They're turning this risky biz into some high-key thrill.

(With that, the CHORUS dips out)

Act 2

Scene 1: Looking For Loverboy

Setting: The Secret Path. A sneaky lane near Capulet's orchard, prime for some covert meet-ups.

(Romeo, looking emo af all alone)

ROMEO *(soliloquizing with a modern twist)*: Bruh, can I really just peace out when my heart's still stuck here? Gotta slide back to where my heart's at.

(ROMEO dips. Enter BENVOLIO and MERCUTIO, decked out like they just stepped off a streetwear runway)

BENVOLIO *(calling out)*: Yo, Romeo, fam, where you at? Romeo, Romeo!

MERCUTIO: My bet? He ghosted straight to his crib, crashed into bed..

BENVOLIO: He zoomed this way, yeeted over this wall. Holler at him, Merc.

MERCUTIO: Watch me work my magic.

(Pauses, listens, but it's crickets)

Romeo! My dude! Mr. Heartbreaker! Romeo! Holler back with a single rhyme, and I'm set. Hit me with an "Ah me!" or maybe drop some bars about "love" and "dove." Throw out a shoutout for our girl Venus. Mention her son Cupid, the OG love sniper.

(Pauses, listens but hears nothing)

Bruh, Romeo's straight up ignoring me. Dude's playing invisible. But watch me lure him out. - I'm calling you out, Romeo, by Rosaline's fire IG feed, by her flawless forehead, those killer red lips, those high-end heels, and them killer legs, and all the heat in that zone. By all   this,   I'm   summoning   you!

(BENVOLIO and MERCUTIO wait for a response, they start emoting.)

BENVOLIO: Man, if Romeo hears all that, he's gonna be heated.

MERCUTIO: Nah, he'd get real salty if I hit up some random to slide into her DMs – that'd get him tight. I'm just spitting facts, using his crush's name to bait him out of his hideout.

BENVOLIO: Homie's probably lurking behind these trees, vibing with the darkness. His love's like that new Netflix show, "Love Is Blind."

MERCUTIO: If love's blind, it can't aim its shot. Now he's gonna camp under a tree, fantasizing his girl was one of those thicc fruits.

(shouting)

Yo, Romeo, bet you're simping hard, wishing she was all about you! Aight, it's a wrap for tonight, Romeo. I'm out. This spot's too chilly for me to crash.

(to BENVOLIO)

Dude lets bounce this is whack.

BENVOLIO: Bet. No use hunting for him if he ain't down to be found.

(BENVOLIO and MERCUTIO exit, leaving the scene with a mix of moods and unanswered calls)

Act 2

Scene 2: Oh Romeo

Setting: *The Iconic Balcony Scene. The ultimate late-night deep convo spot. Romeo's down below, shooting his shot like he's on a dating app.*

(ROMEO, totally smitten, is ready to double-tap that like button)

ROMEO *(whispering to the moonlit night)*: Talking 'bout heartbreak is easy when you've never been left on read.

(JULIET steps onto the balcony, styled like she's about to break the internet)

Sheesh! What's that thirst trap in the window over there? Yo, there's Juliet, looking like a straight up VSCO girlie. Glow, queen, glow! Make the moon hit that 'sksksk'. It's just jelly 'cause you're serving looks that are next level. She's legit my #WCW, no cap. But what's the sitch? Her eyes are spilling the tea, I gotta shoot my shot. But wait, am I being extra? Haven't even snagged a like from her yet. But those eyes, bro, they're like the stars called in sick and asked her peepers to cover the night shift. Imagine her eyes lighting up the sky, the real stars would be throwing shade. If her eyes were up in the heavens, they'd turn the night into Coachella vibes, birds would start chirping, thinking it's daybreak already. Peep her over there, leaning, hand on cheek. Dude, I'm straight up wishing I was that bracelet, just chilling there, up close and personal.

JULIET: Oh my!

(ROMEO watches, totally vibing with JULIET)

ROMEO *(to himself)*: She's speaking now, keep dropping those lines, you baddie. You're out here looking like a Instagram model, high-key making us all look basic, watching you like you're on a live stream.

JULIET *(unaware ROMEO can hear her)*: Oh Romeo, Romeo, why you gotta be a Montague? Drop your dad's name, switch up your profile. Or, if you won't unfollow your fam, just hit me with that "I'm into you," and I'll ghost my Capulet tag!

ROMEO *(to himself)*: Do I keep lurking or just speak up now?

JULIET *(still clueless ROMEO is there)*: It's just your name that's the beef. You'd still be it even if you weren't a Montague. What's in a name, anyway? It ain't like a snap, a story, a tweet, or any other part of your online rep. Yo, be any other handle! What's in a name? That thing we call a rose would still be fire if we called it something else. Romeo would still be Romeo, no cap, even with a different @. Romeo, drop your last name. Trade it—it ain't really you—and in exchange, take all of me.

ROMEO *(to JULIET)*: I'm down with your vibes. Just call me your bae, and I'll cop a new name. From now, Montague is dead to me.

JULIET: Who's creeping? Why you lurking in the shadows, spying on my late-night thoughts? Super sus.

ROMEO: I can't even say who I am. My name, legit, feels like a curse, because it's like being on the rival team to you. If it was a tweet, I'd just delete it.

JULIET: Haven't even heard a hundred words from you, but I already recognize your voice. Aren't you Romeo, and from the Montague fam?

ROMEO: Not if you're not vibing with it, no cap.

JULIET: But how'd you even slide in here? These walls are high-key and not easy to climb. Plus, it's risky AF being here. If any of my squad catches you. It's GG.

ROMEO: I flew over these walls with the wings of love, 'cause love doesn't see limits, it just shoots its shot. Your fam can't stop this vibe.

JULIET: If they spot you, they will yeet you for sure.

ROMEO: One bad look from you is worse for me than your whole squad. Just throw me a smile, and I'm invincible to their hate.

JULIET: I'd be shook if they found you here, no joke.

ROMEO: I'm under the night's cover. If you you're not feelin' me, let them come. Better to end it all than to live without your love.

JULIET: How'd you even find this spot?

ROMEO: It was all for the vine— love showed me the way. Gave me the deets and I just followed. I'm no sailor but I'd sail the farthest sea to slide into your DM's.

JULIET: You can't see, but I'm low-key blushing under this night filter. Normally, I'd be playing it cool, acting hard to get, but forget those games! Are you feeling? On god I know you're gonna say yes. But dudes sometimes ghost, you know? They say the gods laugh at lovers' cringe promises. So, Romeo, if you're feeling it, keep it 100.

Or if you think I'm an easy catch, I'll play hard to get, make you work for it. But fr, I'm all in king. Don't think I'm just being a pick me girl. I might seem forward, but no cap. I should've played it cooler, but you made me catch feels heavy. So, excuse the quickness but it's not just a crush.

ROMEO: On god queen — I swear by the moon. Its light just hits different.

JULIET: Nah, don't swear by the moon, that stan who changes her mood every night. I don't want your feels to be that inconsistent.

ROMEO: So, what should I swear by?

JULIET: Don't swear at all. But if you gotta, swear on yourself king— you're basically my #1. I'd believe that.

ROMEO: If I'm talking real love here…

JULIET: Hold up, I'm into you, but this is all happening too fast. It's like a flash mob, gone before you can even Snap it. Let's just chill. This thing between us could turn into something epic later. Night, night! I hope you enjoy some rest and let me be in my feels.

ROMEO: You're gonna leave me hanging like this?

JULIET: What more do you expect from our late night rendezvous?

ROMEO: Just wanna lock in that you're into me, like I'm into you.

JULIET: I already hit you with my feels before you even asked. On god that's how I feel. Wish I could say it all over again.

ROMEO: This night's hitting different, fam. Feels like I'm living in a dream, way too good to be real.

JULIET: I'm just spilling my tea again. No cap, I'm all about this vibe we got. My love's like an endless scroll — deep and never-ending. The more I'm in your head, the more I vibe, 'cause it's infinite, you know?

NURSE (*from inside*): Juliet!

JULIET: On my way, Nurse! - Hold on, Romeo, if you're just clout chasing, please, I'm begging—

NURSE (*from inside*): Juliet!

JULIET: I'm begging you to stop hitting me up if that's the case. I'll shoot you a message tomorrow.

ROMEO: On god Juliet, I'm high-key serious.

JULIET: Okay then, goodnight, like a thousand times!

(*Juliet dips above*)

ROMEO: Every minute without you feels like a major L.

(*He starts to leave, but Juliet re-enters above*)

JULIET: Wait up, Romeo! I wish I could put your name on blast! Gotta keep it low, or I'd wake the whole block yelling 'ROMEO!' on repeat.

ROMEO: It's like my heart's got notifications on for your voice. Sneaking in these late night chats hit different.

JULIET: Romeo!

ROMEO: Yes?

JULIET: What time should I slide into your DMs tomorrow?

ROMEO: Hit me up at like 9.

JULIET: I won't ghost. Feels like forever till then. Totally spaced why I called you back.

ROMEO: I'll just chill here till you remember.

JULIET: I'll keep forgetting, just to keep you on the line, 'cause I'm living for this moment. It's a whole mood.

ROMEO: And I'm here for it, forgetting the world, just vibing with you.

JULIET: Day's almost breaking. You should probably dip out. But like, stay connected, I need you simping. That clingy vibe.

ROMEO: I'll be doing the most, queen.

JULIET: Same, but I'd probably smother you with all the attention. Wheels up, King! Saying goodbye lowkey sucks, but I'll keep saying night till it's actually morning.

(Juliet dips again)

ROMEO: Hope you catch some good Z's and dream about me. Wish I could sleep next to you, that'd be the ultimate W. Gonna head to my lowkey Friar's spot, need his help and gotta spill about all this hype stuff happening.

(Romeo bounces)

Act 2

Scene 3: BFF Advice

Setting: *Friar Laurence's Herbal Etsy Shop. Friar Laurence's place is an organic, eco-friendly, plant-loving paradise - like an Etsy shop for medieval herbs.*

FRIAR LAWRENCE *(vibing holding a basket)*: Sun's out, guns out, tossing shade at the night like it's outta style. The sky's straight up flexing rn. Night's peacing out quick af. Time to cop some aesthetic herbs and photogenic flowers for the 'gram. Earth's legit the OG influencer: spawns life and snatches it back. It's wild how her kids are all different, sipping on her natural clout. Some plants are like wellness influencers, others just chillin'. Nature's got these hidden hacks in plants and rocks. Everything's got its glow-up moment, but even the chill stuff can turn sus if you're not careful. Stay woke, or things flip to the dark side.

FRIAR LAWRENCE *(vibing holding a basket)*:
Morning's popping up, giving night the side-eye, lighting up the sky with some fire streaks. The dark's staggering out like it partied too

hard, making way for the sun's hot flex. Gotta fill this basket with some edgy weeds and Insta-worthy flowers. Earth's like the ultimate influencer: birthing and burying all at once. It's wild how different her kids are, all sipping on her natural goodness. Some are like wellness gurus, others just cool in their own way. Man, nature's got mad skills hidden in plants and rocks and stuff. Nothing's totally trash, everything's got its glow-up moment. But even the good stuff can turn sus if you use it wrong. Gotta keep it real, or it flips to the dark side.

(Romeo enters)

Even in this tiny flower, there's both poison and healing vibes. Sniff it, and you feel all good; taste it, and it hits different, like, straight to the heart. That's how it goes, in people too — we're all about that mix of chill and wild. And where the bad vibes dominate, it's only a matter of time before everything goes south.

ROMEO:
Ayo, good morning, boomer!

FRIAR LAWRENCE: Who's bringing in the good vibes this early? Kinda sus to be up before the crack of dawn. You got some drama keeping you up, or did you just skip the whole sleep thing?

ROMEO: You got it right. Skipped my bed for something better.

FRIAR LAWRENCE: Sheesh, hope it wasn't trouble! You weren't with Rosaline, were you?

ROMEO: With Rosaline? Nah, Pops. I've swiped left on that. Totally over it.

FRIAR LAWRENCE: Aye, that's what's up. Where were you then?

ROMEO: I'll spill the tea before you even ask. I was vibing with someone from the rival family. Got hit with the feels, and sent them right back. We need a marriage ASAP, and you're the CEO of that.

FRIAR LAWRENCE: I'm hella confused farm. Keep it 100 with me, Romeo. No beating around the bush.

ROMEO: Aight, so here's the DL: I'm hella crushing for Juliet, the daughter of the Capulets. We're both crushing hard, and we're ready to make it IG official with a wedding. I'll spill all the deets about how we met and all that, but for now, I just need your help to make it happen today.

FRIAR LAWRENCE: Whoa young blood, hold up! You just ghosted Rosaline? Young guys seem to fall for what they see, not what they feel. Bruh, you simped so hard over Rosaline! All those emo songs, just for a crush that's not even on your radar anymore? Your Insta stories are still full of indirect sighs over her. You were all about Rosaline, and now you've switched up?

ROMEO: But like you said I was just simping over Rosaline.

FRIAR LAWRENCE: Right, you were obsessed, not in love, my guy.

ROMEO: Facts, and you told me to forget about her.

FRIAR LAWRENCE: I didn't mean for you to ghost her out of nowhere.

ROMEO: Whatever boomer, it is what it is. The girl I'm into now is all about mutual respect and love. Rosaline was just a fling to me.

FRIAR LAWRENCE: Rosaline figured out your game quick, kid. It wasn't genuine. But whatever, young padawan, let's roll. I'll help you out with Juliet. Maybe this toxic love can turn this old family drama into a family reunion.

ROMEO: Periodt, let's bounce. I'm in a major rush here.

FRIAR LAWRENCE: Relax, bro. Rushing usually ends in L's

(They exit)

Act 2

Scene 4: The Boys' Roast Session

Setting: Verona Streets, Gossip Central. The streets of Verona are buzzing with the latest gossip.

(Enter BENVOLIO and MERCUTIO)

MERCUTIO: Yo, where's Romeo hiding? Dude ghosted all night?

BENVOLIO: Nah, checked his crib. He was MIA.

MERCUTIO: Bet it's Rosaline's ghosting that's got him all emo.

BENVOLIO: Tybalt, from the Capulet squad, slid a letter into Romeo's DMs.

MERCUTIO: Def a throwdown invite.

BENVOLIO: Romeo's gonna clap back, for sure.

MERCUTIO: Anyone can hit reply.

BENVOLIO: Romeos should put him on blast.

MERCUTIO: Bruh, Romeo's already been KO'd by Rosaline's cold heart, Cupid's arrow did him dirty. And now he's gonna step up to Tybalt?

BENVOLIO: What's Tybalt even like?

MERCUTIO: High-key, the dude's a real try-hard, the 'Prince of Cats'. Steezy af, hitting beats like he's in a rap battle. Dude's all about finesse. This Tybalt's like the final boss, a master of dueling. He's got these fancy moves, the passado, the reverse stab. It's like he's doing TikTok dances in a fight.

BENVOLIO: The what now?

MERCUTIO: I'm so done with these wannabe influencers, always flexing their latest drip. Its cringe af. Isn't it just tragic how they can't even chill without flexing? It's all about the aesthetic, never about the real talk.

(Romeo vibes in)

BENVOLIO: Look, Romeo's finally showing up.

MERCUTIO: Looking all drained, like he lost his vibe. Dude's been deep in the feels, spitting poetry like he's the new Petrarch. All those classic babes — Laura, Dido, Cleopatra, Helen, Hero, Thisbe — they're just basic compared to his girl. Romeo, what's up! Dropping a French 'hello' to match your swag from last night. You totally bailed on us, man.

ROMEO: Hey, good morning guys. What do you mean I bailed on you?

MERCUTIO: You straight-up ghosted us, man. Can't deny.

ROMEO: My bad, Mercutio, On god, I had major stuff going down. Iykyk. It be like that sometimes.

MERCUTIO: So in other words you ditched us for a baddie with a truck in the back.

ROMEO: Like, dump truck?

MERCUTIO: A dump truck with a lift.

ROMEO: Facts. Several points were made.

MERCUTIO: Bruh I'm king of finesse. Don't forget that.

ROMEO: You're actually the king of deez.

MERCUTIO: Deez?

ROMEO: Deez nuts.

MERCUTIO: Bruh, if that's all you got, take several seats. You're cringe no cap.

ROMEO: I think you're just salty you couldn't clap back.

MERCUTIO: Benvolio, jump in, I need a break.

ROMEO: Don't quit on me now king, you don't want me taking the W right?

MERCUTIO: If we're going back to memes I'm out fam.

ROMEO: What do you mean you're a meme lord, Mercutio.

MERCUTIO: Gonna have to roast you back for that one.

ROMEO: Chill, don't get salty king!

MERCUTIO: Your jokes are funny but savage. That's some spicy banter.

ROMEO: Perfect for a fire meme, right?

MERCUTIO: Haha, Isn't this such a mood compared to simping over someone? Now you're the life of the chat, the real Romeo. That lovesick mode was super extra...

BENVOLIO: Yo, hit the brakes on that, that's enough.

MERCUTIO: You want me to stop when it's just heating up?

BENVOLIO: Or else you'd never stop.

MERCUTIO: Nah fam, you're trippin'. I was about to drop the mic, was at the climax of my story.

(Enter Nurse and her man Peter)

ROMEO: Yo, check who just popped up.

BENVOLIO: We got company!

MERCUTIO: Squad goals - it's the iconic duo.

NURSE: Peter!

PETER: Right here!

NURSE: My fan, Peter.

MERCUTIO: Peter, use that fan to cover her face; the fan's got more game.

NURSE: Hey, good morning, guys.

MERCUTIO: And a fine evening to you, ma'am.

NURSE: Evening, already?

MERCUTIO: Nah, it's high-key the peak of the day.

NURSE: Oh, come on! What kind of guy are you?

MERCUTIO: Just a regular dude, but God threw in some extra spice..

NURSE: Ha! That's one way to put it. Hey, do any of you know where I can find lil Romeo?

ROMEO: That's me, but I'll be older by the time you find me than when you started looking. I'm the latest version, just dropped.

NURSE: You're not wrong.

MERCUTIO: Oh, is being the 'worst' the new trend? Smooth, Romeo.

NURSE *(to ROMEO)*: If you're Romeo, I need a sec to chat.

BENVOLIO: Watch out, she's sliding into your DMs with a dinner invite.

MERCUTIO: What a plot twist, a total game changer!

ROMEO: What's the tea?

MERCUTIO: Nothing major unless it's like finding a cringe meme in your feed. Just recycling old trends.

(sings)

An old trend, so old,
Still cool for a throwback.
But a trend that's too stale,
Is a flop, can't prevail

When it's past its viral comeback.

Romeo, rolling to your dad's? We're grabbing lunch there.

ROMEO: Sounds like a plan, I'm in.

MERCUTIO: Peace out, fam!

(Mercutio and Benvolio exit)

NURSE: So, who was that edgy dude, throwing all that shade?

ROMEO: Just a guy who loves the sound of his own voice, spitting more in a minute than he'd back up in a month.

NURSE *(to Peter)*: And you just let him diss me?

PETER: I didn't catch any disrespect. If I did, I'd have been ready to go viral for you, no joke. I'm not scared to clap back if it's legit.

NURSE: I'm low-key shook right now.

(to Romeo)

Can we spill some tea? My girl sent me to scope you out. What she told me to say, I'll keep on the DL. But real talk, if you're playing her, leading her on, that's mad sus. She's young, so playing games with her would be totally not cool.

ROMEO: Nurse, tell Juliet I'm all in. On god...

NURSE: For real, I'll tell her that, and she's gonna be on cloud nine.

ROMEO: What exactly will you tell her, Nurse? I hope you've understood the assignment.

NURSE: I'll tell her you're down for it, which is pretty chill of you.

ROMEO: Tell her to find a way to sneak out this afternoon. She'll meet me at Friar Lawrence's place to get hitched.

(throws some coins at her)

Here's some cash for your trouble.

NURSE: No need for your cash, but thanks.

ROMEO: Come on, take it.

NURSE: This afternoon, huh? Alright, she'll be there.

(picks up 35 coins from the ground)

ROMEO: And hold up, Nurse. In about an hour, my guy will meet you behind the abbey with some ropes set up like stairs. We will use that to climb the walls to reach Juliet.

NURSE: I gotchu, but I have a question.

ROMEO: Dope! What's up?

NURSE: Is your guy low-key? Ever heard, "Two can't keep a secret if one of them is out of the loop"?

ROMEO: Facts, my guy's solid as they come.

NURSE: Well, let me tell you, my girl J is the sweetest. Back when she was just a little chatterbox... Oh, and there's this dude, Paris, trying to slide into her DMs, but she's like 'eww', would rather chill with a frog than him. I troll her sometimes, saying Paris is the better catch. But man, when I say that, she goes as white as a ghost. Isn't it funny how both 'rosemary' and 'Romeo' start with an R?

ROMEO: Yeah, so? They both start with R.

NURSE: LOL, you're clowning. R is for... wait, it starts with something else. She's got this cute way of linking you and rosemary, you'd be shook to hear it.

ROMEO: Pass on my 'hey' to your girl.

NURSE: For sure, like a thousand times. - Peter!

PETER: Yeah?

NURSE *(giving PETER her fan)***:** Let's roll out fam.

(They all dip)

Act 2

Scene 5: Big Moves

Setting: The Capulet's Insta-Worthy Garden. Juliet's backyard is looking like a viral Instagram garden, decked out with fairy lights, aesthetic plants, and a cozy swing.

JULIET *(bouncing in, hyped):* I hit up my girl to find Romeo at like, 9 AM. Is she lost or something? No way, she's just taking forever! Ugh, she's moving like a bad connection! Love's messengers should be like 5G, zooming faster than a viral meme. They should be like influencers, flocking to a new brunch spot. Now it's noon, that's three hours since 9, and she's still MIA. If she was feeling the vibe, she'd be rapid, like typing on fire. My messages would bounce to her, and she'd be pinging them straight to Romeo and back to me. But boomers can be like buffering videos: slow and laggy.

(Nurse and Peter slide in)

Oh, finally! Nurse, what's good? Peter, can you ghost for a sec?

NURSE: Peter, go guard the door.

(PETER leaves)

JULIET: Aight, Nurse, spill the tea! Wait, why you looking all moody? If it's L news, drop it lightly on me. Why are you looking beat?

NURSE: Girl, I'm beat. Gimme a minute, will ya? My bones are finessing me. I've been running all over.

JULIET: If I had your tired bones and your news, I'd be chillin'. Spill it, Nurse, what's the deal?

NURSE: Oof, you're so thirsty for the tea! Don't you see I'm outta breath?

JULIET: How can you be outta breath and still talking about being outta breath? You're giving me more excuses than actual news. Is it good or bad? Just spill!

NURSE: Girl, your taste in guys is, like, questionable. Romeo? Though his face is like #NoFilter needed, and he's got some nice legs. His hands, feet, and bod aren't all that – but also kinda are. He's not Mr. Manners 2024, but, for real, he's as sweet as a puppy. Anyway, do your thing. How's it going? Eaten anything yet?

JULIET: Nah, no snack yet. You're just hitting me with old news. What's up with our wedding plans?

NURSE: Ugh, my head's killing me. Feels like it's gonna explode into a million pieces. And my back is blown out!

(JULIET rubs her back)

JULIET: Yo Nurse, you're my real MVP, always hustling. But for real, did my main squeeze Romeo slide into your DMs with any deets?

NURSE: Girl, your bae is all legit. Like, CEO of Chivalry and stuff. But hey, where's your mom at?

JULIET: Mom? She's chilling inside. Why you asking all weird? You're like, "Your boo, Mr. Perfect, is like...'Yo, where's your mom?'"

NURSE: Lord, have mercy! Girl, you're more extra than my data charges. You think me spilling tea is gonna fix my backache? Next time, slide into his DMs yourself.

JULIET: Chill, Nurse. You're the one being extra. What's the word from Romeo?

NURSE: Got the green light to hit up confession today?

JULIET: Totally.

NURSE: Then yeet over to Friar Lawrence's pad. Your future hubby's there, ready to put a ring on it. Look at you, blushing like you just got a shoutout. Off to church, girl. I gotta sneak off to snag a ladder.
Romeo's gonna climb up to your crib tonight. I'm out here doing the grunt work for your happily ever after. But hey, pretty soon you'll be busy doing all that wifey stuff, know what I mean? I'm off to grab some lunch. You, go meet Friar Lawrence.

JULIET: Rushing to my epic win! Thanks a mil, ur a real one. Catch you later!

(They dip fast af)

Act 2

Scene 6: The Stealth Wedding

Setting: *Friar Lawrence's Chapel. There's an altar up front, all set for Romeo and Juliet's hush-hush "I dos".*

FRIAR LAWRENCE: Romeo let's hope the universe is vibing with this wedding, so we don't end up with major regrets later.

ROMEO: Facts. No drama's gonna kill the vibe I get from just seeing Juliet. Let's lock this down. Even if we crash and burn, I'm down for it. Making her mine is the ultimate goal.

FRIAR LAWRENCE: Easy there, Romeo. Instant love's like a firework – lit and loud, but burns out fast. It's like that with too much of anything, even love. Don't rush the plot.

(JULIET enters like she just hit 1M followers and hug ROMEO)

And here's your girl. Juliet, you're floating like a cloud emoji, but life's road is tough like a bad Wi-Fi connection. Love's light, like a perfect selfie filter – feels epic, but doesn't always last. That's the real talk with these heart emojis.

JULIET: Hey there, my brother in Christ!

FRIAR LAWRENCE: I bet Romeo's gonna hit you with the 'thanks a million' for both of us.

JULIET: I'll hit him back with the same thanks. Gotta keep it 100.

ROMEO: Juliet, if you're feeling as hyped as I am and you've got the words, let's make some #RelationshipGoals.
JULIET: Romeo, my brain's buzzing with more feels than I can text out. It's like trying to count your followers when they're blowing up. Your love's made me so rich, counting it all is a lost cause.

FRIAR LAWRENCE: Aight, let's get this show on the road. I'm not leaving you two alone until you're officially #Married. Time to lock this down.

(FRIAR LAWRENCE marries ROMEO and JULIET Alexa play Marry You by Bruno Mars)

Act 3: The Plot Thickens
Scene 1: The Showdown Goes Viral

Setting: The streets of Verona, looking like the main strip of the city. Think modern urban vibes: cool cafes, graffiti art, and the buzz of people everywhere. (Enter Benvolio and Mercutio, strutting onto the scene like they're about to drop a new yeezy album)

BENVOLIO: Mercutio, bro, let's dip out. It's blazing hot and the Capulets are lurking. If we bump into them, it's gonna be World War III.

MERCUTIO: You're like one of those dudes who slams his blade on the bar and is like, "Hope I don't have to use this." Two drinks later, he's swinging it at the bartender for literally no reason.

BENVOLIO: For real? Am I that guy?

MERCUTIO: Dude, you could win the 'Most Likely to Rage' award in Italy. Someone breathes wrong, and you're ready to throw down. Looking for a fight? You'll find one, trust me.

BENVOLIO: And?

MERCUTIO: If there were two of you, Verona would need a backup Benvolio. You'd beef with a guy for having one more or one less beard hair than you. Or start drama over nut-cracking 'cause your eyes got that nutty vibe. Your head's like a 24/7 fight club, no cap. Remember when you beefed with a guy for coughing? Or got salty with your tailor for styling you out of season? And let's not forget the shoelace incident. And now you're playing the peacemaker?

BENVOLIO: No way bro, if I was as fight happy as you, my life insurance would be through the roof.

MERCUTIO: Life insurance? Now you're just tripping.

(TYBALT, PETRUCHIO, and the CAPULETS roll up)

BENVOLIO: Oh, look who it is – the Capulet squad.

MERCUTIO: Whatever, I'm not sweating it.

TYBALT (to PETRUCHIO and the others): Stay on my six, I'll handle this.

(to the MONTAGUES)

'Sup, guys. I need a word with one of you.

MERCUTIO:

Just one word? Why not make it a word and catch these hands?

TYBALT: You want beef?

MERCUTIO: Do I need to spoon-feed you a reason?

TYBALT: You're rolling with Romeo, aren't you?

MERCUTIO: Benvolio, they think we're some boy band, ready to drop a beat? Nah, fam. This right here (touches his side) ain't a mic, it's my heat. 'Bout to make 'em dance to a whole new beat.

BENVOLIO: Bars. But chill Mercutio, were out in the open. Let's either find a spot to hash this out on the low, or just bounce. Everyone's got their eyes on us right now.

MERCUTIO: Eyes are meant for peeping the scene, so let 'em watch. Ain't nobody gonna make me dip.

(ROMEO enters)

TYBALT: Peace, but only 'cause my main dude just rolled up. What's good, Romeo?

MERCUTIO: That ain't your dude. Sure, take a stroll in the field, he might follow. That's the only way he's your "man".

TYBALT: Romeo, we got mad beef.

ROMEO: Tybalt, for real, I got reasons to not beef with you, reasons that cool my temper and brush off that diss. I ain't no villain. So, deuces. You don't even know what's up.

TYBALT: Boy, your words can't fix your actions. Time to turn up and pull out your strap.

ROMEO: Bruh, you got it twisted. I never wronged you. I got love for you, more than you know, till you get why I do. So, cool it, Capulet - a name I respect like my own. You should be straight with what I'm saying.

MERCUTIO: This is weak, fam. Time to end this soft play. (pulls out his strap) Tybalt, the ultimate rat-catcher, you down to clash?

TYBALT: What's up then?

MERCUTIO: Oh, King of Cats, I'm here to snatch one of your nine lives. I'll take one, and depending on how you play it, might just knock the rest outta you. Your bussy is mine. You gonna pull out your piece or what? Make it quick, or I'll be on you with my piece before you even draw.

TYBALT: Let's go then. (he draws his strap)

ROMEO: Mercutio, my guy, put that away!

MERCUTIO *(to TYBALT)*: Let's see your moves, bruh.

(MERCUTIO and TYBALT fight)

ROMEO *(drawing his piece)*: Benvolio, get your strap out. We gotta shut down their heat. Cut it out, both of you! Tybalt, Mercutio, the Prince banned street fights in Verona. Chill, Tybalt. Cool it, Mercutio!

(ROMEO tries to break up the fight. TYBALT sneaks a shot under ROMEO'S arm, hitting MERCUTIO)

PETRUCHIO: Oh snap. Let's dip, Tybalt!

(TYBALT, PETRUCHIO, and the other CAPULETS bounce quick af)

MERCUTIO: I'm hit... On god I'll haunt you all I swear. Did he get away without a scratch?

ROMEO: You good, Mercutio!?

MERCUTIO: Lowkey just a nick, but it's enough., Where's my page? Go, fetch a doc, stat!

(MERCUTIO'S PAGE runs off)

ROMEO: Stay strong, fam. It's not that bad.

MERCUTIO: Nobody makes me bleed my own blood! Nah, not as deep as a well, or as broad as a church door, but it's enough. It's the endgame for me. Check for me tomorrow, and you'll find me a goner. I'm done in this world, for real. May a curse hit both your houses! Dang! Can't believe that dog, that rat, that mouse, that cat took me out! That show-off, punk villain, fighting like he's straight outta Compton! Why'd you even jump in? He got me while I was under your arm.

ROMEO: I thought I was doing the right thing. RIP!

MERCUTIO (*stumbling*): Benvolio, get me inside somewhere, fam, or I'm legit gonna pass out. A plague on both your houses! Lowkey I'll be 6 feet under soon. I'm finna check out. Curse you all!

(*MERCUTIO and BENVOLIO slowly walk away*)

ROMEO: Bruh, Mercutio, my cousin from the Prince's fam and my day one, just got clapped defending me from Tybalt's heat Oh, Juliet, your love's got me feeling all twisted, big oof!

(*BENVOLIO enters*)

BENVOLIO (*makes a slicing motion over his neck*): Romeo, man, Mercutio's gone. His brave spirit's flying up to heaven, but dude left the chat way too soon.

ROMEO: Today's L is just the start. What popped off today's gonna spark a whole vibe of terror down the line.

(*TYBALT enters*)

BENVOLIO: Tybalt's rolling back in.

ROMEO: And there's Tybalt, rolling back like he's the CEO of murder, and Mercutio's dead? Time to switch from chill to beast mode. Tybalt, you called me "villain" earlier. Well, That clapback you hit me with, Tybalt, it's about to get real. Mercutio's spirit's just up there, waiting for some company. It's either you, me, or both of us joining him.

TYBALT: You, that emo boy hanging with Mercutio, you're gonna join him now.

ROMEO: This is where we find out fam.

(They scrap. TYBALT gets iced by ROMEO)

BENVOLIO: Romeo, you gotta bounce, now! The whole block's waking up, and Tybalt's down. Don't just stand there shook. The Prince will have your head if you get caught. Ghost, my dude, ghost!

ROMEO: He couldn't take the clap back!

BENVOLIO: Bruh why you still here, fam?

(Enter CITIZENS OF THE WATCH)

CITIZEN OF THE WATCH: Who dipped after dropping Mercutio? Where's Tybalt?

BENVOLIO: Tybalt's right there, ded AF.

CITIZEN OF THE WATCH: (to TYBALT) Get up, bro, you're coming with me. I'm charging you in the Prince's name, let's roll.

(TYBALT obviously dead, does not move)

(Exit ROMEO)

(Enter PRINCE, MONTAGUE, CAPULET, LADY MONTAGUE, LADY CAPULET, and a bunch of randoms)

PRINCE: Where they at? The ones who sparked this mess?

BENVOLIO: Yo, Prince, I got the full scoop on this beef. Right there's Tybalt, iced. He murked Mercutio, and then young Romeo clapped him back.

LADY CAPULET: That's my nephew, Tybalt! My brother's own kid! Oh Prince, my man, my husband! My nephew's gone! Prince, you gotta do right by us. Serve up some justice on the Montagues. Oh cousin, cousin!

PRINCE: Benvolio, who kicked off this clash?

BENVOLIO: It was Tybalt, before Romeo got to him. Romeo was all respectful, telling Tybalt this whole drama was wack. He was like, "Prince ain't gonna vibe with this." He said it all chill, even took a knee, showing mad respect. But Tybalt was all heated, wasn't hearing any peace talk. Then Tybalt and Mercutio got into it, wildin' out, going at each other hard. Romeo was shouting, "Yo, cut it out, bros. Chill." Jumped right in to break it up, made them drop their straps. But Tybalt sneaked a hit on Mercutio under Romeo's arm, then he dipped out fast. But real quick, Tybalt came back, and Romeo was already high-key on that revenge vibe. They clashed like lightning, and before anyone could break it up, Tybalt was down. Romeo dipped the moment Tybalt hit the ground. On my life, I'm spitting facts here.

LADY CAPULET: Prince, don't listen to him. Benvolio's Montague squad deep, so he's capping. He ain't spilling the real tea. It was like twenty Montagues on one, and they still only dropped Tybalt. I want justice, Prince. Romeo took out Tybalt. Romeo's gotta pay with his life.

PRINCE: Tybalt took Mercutio. Romeo took Tybalt. Who's gonna answer for Mercutio now?

MONTAGUE: Nah, Prince, not Romeo. He was Mercutio's fam. He just did what justice should've done, by taking out Tybalt.

PRINCE: For that, Romeo's getting exiled from Verona. This beef's hit home for me too. Mercutio was my kin, and now he's gone 'cause of your fam feud. My punishment's gonna be so harsh, you'll wish you never crossed me. I ain't here for your excuses or prayers. Romeo bounces from Verona ASAP, or he's done for. Get Tybalt outta here, and do as I say. Showing mercy to killers just breeds more violence.

(They exit)

Act 3

Scene 2: Waiting On Read

Setting: *Juliet's bedroom. Its stage of suspense and high emotion. Lots of anxiety frfr.*

JULIET *(chilling solo, daydreaming)*: Sun, can you not? Just hit that logout already! I'm so here for night mode. That's when Romeo slides into my DMs, lowkey. Night's like the ultimate wingman for love, you feel? It's all about those feels you can't see. Love's either playing blind man's bluff or just goes all in when the lights are out. I'm over here like, 'Night, let's get this show on the road, decked out in your darkest emo drip.' Gotta upgrade to official bae status, you get me? In the dark, nobody's gonna see me blushing. This shy girl's gotta level up her love game, keep it 100 but still cute. Yo, Night, you better step on it and bring my Romeo along. Dude shines brighter in the dark than like, snow on a crow's back. Roll up, night. Deliver my Romeo. And when he dips, turn him into a star, make him go viral. He'll make the night sky so fire, everyone's gonna be stanning the night, straight up ghosting daytime. I've got this love thing down, but still waiting to go all in. Romeo's tagged as mine, but we haven't gone Insta official. This day's dragging on forever, like waiting for that hype drop, can't wait to rock my new look.

(as she spots the NURSE coming)

Oh, here's my main with the update. Every time Romeo's name drops, it's like a bop. Nurse, what's good? Is that the rope ladder Romeo was gonna send?

NURSE: Yep, this is it.

JULIET: Hold up, why you looking so shook? Spill the tea, what's going down?

NURSE: Girl, it's a big yikes! He's done. He's dead. Talk about an L day. RIP Tybalt.

JULIET: Is this for real? Is the universe being this hella sus?

NURSE: Romeo's the sus one here. Oh, Romeo, Romeo, who would've thought it'd be him?

JULIET: Are you straight-up messing with me? This is like being dragged through hell. Did Romeo yeet himself? Just say "yes" and I'll be more salty than a sea snake. If Romeo's offed himself, I'm done for. If he's murked, say "yes." If not, drop a "no." Your words are gonna vibe check my whole life.

NURSE: I saw it, girl, right on his manly chest. It's all facts, no cap. A real tragic scene, a bloody, heartbreaking sight.

JULIET: That's so zooted! Pale and soaked in blood? All that dried-up blood looking mad gory. I'm dead, just thinking about it.

NURSE: Girl, your heart's breaking. Like, it's going bankrupt with sadness. You're talking 'bout locking up your eyes, never letting them peep anything again. You're ready to just yeet your body back to the earth, not moving again. Laying down with Romeo in one tragic coffin.

JULIET: Oh, Tybalt, my day one, the realest homie I had. Such a legit dude, Tybalt, an honorable guy for real. Wish I didn't have to see him drop like that.

NURSE: It's all bad, Juliet. Romeo's dipped, and Tybalt's gone too. Tybalt was your main cuz, but Romeo, your man, meant even more. We might as well play some doom tunes, 'cause if they're both out, who's left?

JULIET: So, Tybalt's straight-up dead, and Romeo's been canceled? Romeo clapped Tybalt and got hit with that exile?

NURSE:
Yeah, he did. Biggest L.

JULIET: That's so sus! Romeo's like a snake rocking flower drip. Ever seen a dragon chilling in a beautiful spot like that? He's a killer cutie, a devil with an angel's face. He's like a raven decked out in dove feathers. A lamb that's lowkey a wolf. I can't even with him, but he looked like the Top G. Total flip of the script, a saint acting all damned, a villain posing as a hero. Nature, why you playing games in hell like that? Why'd you make him catch a case? Was there ever such a messed-up story hidden behind such a fire post? I just can't deal with the fact that so much evil was lurking in something so goated!

NURSE: No cap, you can't trust guys. They're all about playing games, faking it. Ugh, where's my guy? I need a drink. This drama's aging me big time. Romeo's gotta get what's coming to him.

JULIET: Hold up, don't be throwing shade on him! He's not about that life. Shame can't even touch him; he's all about the honor. I was trippin' over him, totally my bad.

NURSE: You're gonna back the dude who clapped your cousin?

JULIET: Should trash talk my own boo? My poor Romeo, who's gonna praise you if your own wife talks trash? But for real, Romeo, why'd you have to ice my cuz? Maybe 'cause Tybalt, the opp, would've done Romeo dirty. I can't even cry about it. I'm happy that Romeo's still breathing, but then I remember Tybalt's not, and it's a huge L. My man, who Tybalt was out to get, is alive. Tybalt, who was gunning for my man, is gone. That's low-key comforting, right? So why am I so salty? But there's something even more out of pocket than Tybalt being gone. Something that's got me wanting to check out. I'd love to forget it, but it's living rent-free in my head, like guilt does in a shady mind. "Tybalt's gone, and Romeo's been cancelled." That banishment is like getting perma'd out of a twitch chat. Just Tybalt being dead is a big enough L. Seems like pain loves company, always rolling up with more. Would've been less of a vibe kill if she just said, "Tybalt's out," and maybe dropped that my folks were gone too. I could've dealt with the usual feels then. But hitting me with "Tybalt's gone, and Romeo's cancelled"? That's like saying my dad, mom, Tybalt, Romeo, and even me are all dead. "Romeo's been cancelled" is like infinite Ls. No cap, no words can touch this pain. Whats my fams take Nurse?

NURSE: They're all salty over Tybalt. Want me to take you to them?

JULIET: They're crying for Tybalt? I'll cry for Romeo's banishment when they're done. Snag those ropes. Joke's on us, right? They were supposed to be for our meetup, but now I'm like a single widow. Let's go, ropes. Come on, Nurse. Off to my wedding bed where it's gonna be death, not Romeo, who takes my single status.

NURSE: Hit your bedroom. I'll scoop up Romeo to cheer you up. I got the deets on his spot. Your Romeo's gonna pull up tonight. He's low-key chilling in Friar Lawrence's spot.

JULIET *(handing over a ring)*: Oh, fr, find him! Slide him this ring, tell my main man to roll up here. He's gotta drop one last 'see ya later alligator' before he dips for good.

(They dip)

Act 3

Scene 3: Major Oof

Setting: *Friar Lawrence's humble cell, its a small, unassuming space with bare stone walls, dimly lit by a candle flickering on a wooden table. Major monk vibes.*

FRIAR LAWRENCE *(to himself)*: Romeo, come on, you're giving bad luck vibes, like you and trouble are a thing now.

(Romeo enters)

ROMEO: Friar, what's DL? What's the Prince's saying? What kind of situation am I in chief?

FRIAR LAWRENCE: Bruh, you got some major bad luck. Got some news about the Prince's decision.

ROMEO: What's he dropping, like doomsday-level stuff?

FRIAR LAWRENCE: Nah, it's not the ultimate L. No execution, just catching a lifetime ban.

ROMEO: Banishment? Bruh, might as well call it an execution. Being exiled hits different, way worse IMO. Say you're joking please!

FRIAR LAWRENCE: That's the tea fam. You're canceled in Verona. Chill though, the world's got mad space.

ROMEO: On god outside these walls is depressing af. Being 'banned' is like losing your Fortnite account. Banishment is legit death, just sugarcoated.

FRIAR LAWRENCE: Oh, that's hella negative, bro. Mad ungrateful! Our rules say it's a wrap for you, but the Prince, being chill, dodged the rule for you. He flipped 'game over' into 'just banned.' That's a solid, and you're not even vibing with it.

ROMEO: Nah, it's straight-up torture, not a solid. Heaven's where Juliet's at. Every random critter gets to stay in heaven here and see her, but not me. I'm like an insignificant Twitch viewer now. Just a number on a screen. You're still saying being banned for life isn't a total L? You couldn't hook me up with something quick, like a poison or a sharp blade, instead of hitting me with 'banished'? That word's cursed, man! It's like the soundtrack of hell. How can you, all holy and stuff, hit me with 'banished'?

FRIAR LAWRENCE: Chill my guy, just listen for a sec.

ROMEO: Bruh, you're gonna hit me with that "banished" talk again, fam?

FRIAR LAWRENCE: Romeo, I got something to shield you from that word. I'm talking 'bout philosophy, the real MVP. It's gonna comfort you, even though you're like, totally banished.

ROMEO: Bruh, you still on that "banished" trip? Nah, skip that philosophy stuff. It gave me no Eagle Powers! Unless it can whip up

Juliet, teleport a whole town, or flip the script on the prince's ban, it's just noise. Zip it chief.

FRIAR LAWRENCE: Oh, so you just gonna not listen to me? Big L.

ROMEO: How's a madman hear if a wiseman can't even see?

FRIAR LAWRENCE: Romeo, let me school you young blood.

ROMEO: You can't school me on feels you ain't feeling, bruh. If you were as young as me, crushing on Juliet, just tied the knot an hour ago, then you offed Tybalt, all lovesick like me, and got slapped with a banish? Then, maybe you could talk. You'd be yanking your hair out and hitting the deck just like I'm doing now.

(ROMEO drops to the ground)

You'd be on your knees, measuring out your own grave that ain't even dug yet.

(Knocking offstage)

FRIAR LAWRENCE: Romeo, get up. Someone's knocking. Hide out my guy.

ROMEO: I'm not hiding! Let me be emo rn!

(ROMEO starts singing I Miss You by Blink 182)

FRIAR LAWRENCE: Ayo, they're still knocking!

(To the door)

Who's that?

(To ROMEO)

Romeo, get up, they're gonna cuff you.

(To the door)

Chill for a sec!

(To ROMEO)

Bruh, get up!

(Knocking)

Hurry, dip into my study!

(To the door)

Hold up - for real, why you gotta be like this? I'm coming, I'm coming!

(Knocking)

Why are you banging on the door all sus like that? Who are you with? What do you want?

NURSE *(Offstage)*: Lemme in, and I'll spill the tea! I'm sliding in for Lady Juliet.

FRIAR LAWRENCE *(to the door)*: Aight, cool, come through.

(NURSE enters)

NURSE: Top G, spill the tea, where's my lady's boo? Where's Romeo at?

Friar Lawrence: He's right there on the floor, being emo AF.

NURSE: Oh snap, he's mirroring Juliet, exactly like her. Oh, this is straight-up tragic! Juliet's doing the same, emo vibes. Romeo, get up! Be a man for Juliet. For her, stand up. Why you gotta kill the vibe?

ROMEO: Nurse! Ugh, IYKYK.

NURSE: Yeah, yeah. Look, everyone's ticket gets punched someday.

ROMEO: Are you bringing news of Juliet? How is she? Does she see me as a straight-up villain now cause I stained our fresh love by icing her cuz? Where is she? How's she holding up? What's my low-key wife saying 'bout our love story gone south?

NURSE: Bruh, she ain't saying nothing, just crying a river. She hits the bed, tries to stand, then shouts "Tybalt!" and goes "Romeo!" before crashing down again. Does not pass the vibe check rn.

ROMEO: She's shouting my name like I'm the bullet that took him out. Friar, where in my body is my name hiding? Point it out so I can carve it out.

(He whips out his emo dagger)

FRIAR LAURENCE: Whoa, chill, bro! Put that dagger away young blood! You're all up in your feelings right now. Listen, your lady still loves you, man. She's just mad salty about Tybalt, that's all. And you? You're alive, fam! Tybalt wanted to ghost you, but you're still here. Juliet's still your girl. The Prince just exiled you, not sent you to meet your maker. There's still hope, dude!

ROMEO: Hope? Bruh, you trippin'. Lifetime ban is worse than death, trust me! It's like you're telling me to go catch some air outside Verona's walls. Nah, fam, there ain't no life outside Juliet. You're saying there's hope, but that's just straight-up cap.

FRIAR LAURENCE: Man, you gotta check yourself before you wreck yourself! You're sounding extra right now. Look, you need to dip out of here and lay low in Mantua. I'll send updates about Juliet and how things are playing out here. Just keep your phone on and wait for my texts. You've got a love story to live for, Romeo. Don't throw it away over some temporary heat.

NURSE: He's right, Romeo. Bounce outta here and get your head straight. Juliet's gonna be all good. I'll slide over to her and drop the 411 about you being okay. But for real, Romeo, you gotta ghost from Verona ASAP.

ROMEO: Aight, I hear you. I'll hit the road to Mantua. But this ain't over chief, not by a long shot. Keep me posted, Friar. Juliet's my heart, fam. Without her, it's like my feed without Wi-Fi – straight up dead zone.

FRIAR LAURENCE: Hold up Romeo! You acting all kinds of sus right now. You're a man, right? But you're out here crying like you lost your blue checkmark. Your moves are so cringe, like you're throwing a fit on a live stream. Man, you're looking more like an old meme than a man, or like some weird Snapchat filter gone wrong. I'm shook, bro. I thought you had more game than this. You iced Tybalt, you wanna ghost yourself, and you thinking 'bout leaving your main squeeze Juliet in the dust? Bruh, why you tripping over life itself? You're supposed to be the CEO of your life, but here you are, acting like you got zero likes. Your body's like an unused gym membership, bro. Your love's like a ghosted text, left on read. And your brain? Man, it's like you forgot the Wi-Fi password. You're like a noob playing Call of Duty, accidentally fragging yourself. Juliet's still your bae, and you're sweating over being exiled? Tybalt was out for your clout, but you clapped him first. Be thankful you ain't in a coffin! The law could've yeeted you, but it just hit you with the block. Your life's got more ups than followers. So, don't be all salty and extra. Slide into Juliet's DMs and hit her with some love. But bro, dip out before the curfew hits, or you won't make it to Mantua. We'll sort your drama, get the Prince to unblock you, and you'll be back with more hype than your fave influencer. Nurse, go tell Juliet her man's coming.

NURSE: For real, I could vibe here all night with this wisdom. Aight, I'll let Juliet know her man's on the way.

ROMEO: Do that and tell her to get ready for some real talk.

NURSE: Here, she sent you this ring.

(gives ROMEO JULIET'S ring, its a ring pop)

Better hustle, it's getting late.

(Exit NURSE)

ROMEO: Yo, this ring just boosted my mood like a fire playlist. LFG.

FRIAR LAURENCE: Aight, Romeo, time to dip. Night, fam. You gotta be slick about this, either bounce before the night crew rolls in, or hit the road in some low-key drip at dawn. Take a little vacay in Mantua. I'll holla at your homie to keep you updated with the 411 on your situation here. Lemme get some dap, bro. It's getting late. Peace out. Good night.

ROMEO: I'm heading out to catch those feels with Juliet, the ultimate high. But on god, it's kinda whack having to ghost you like this. Wheels up King.

(They all dip)

Act 3

Scene 4: Midnight Meeting

Setting: The Capulet's living room, which could double as a set for a reality TV show. Imagine plush sofas, dramatic lighting, and a vibe that screams 'money'.

CAPULET: Man, life's wildin out rn, no joke. We haven't even hype up our girl for marrying you, Paris. Just so you know, she was super tight with Tybalt, and now she's all in her feels. It's late, she's not coming down tonight. Straight up, if you weren't here, I'd be snoozing already.

PARIS: For real, these times are a mood killer. Night, fam. Tell Juliet I said 'hey'.

LADY CAPULET: Fo' sho, I'll get the deets on her thoughts about getting hitched by tomorrow. Tonight, she's locked up in her room, all up in her feels.

CAPULET: Paris, I'm gonna hype her up big time for you. Bet she'll vibe with what I say. No doubt. My wife, drop by her room before you crash, talk up Paris's love game. Check it, on Wednesday— what day we on again?

PARIS : Monday, my dude.

CAPULET: Monday, right. Wednesday's way too soon. Let's do Thursday. So, on Thursday, break it down for her: she's getting hitched to our boy, the earl. You down with that? Think it's too rushed? We can't go all out with the party vibes – just keep it low-key. Tybalt just got clapped, so we can't flex too hard and disrespect his memory. Let's keep it chill, maybe invite a small squad, like six peeps max. You cool with Thursday?

PARIS: Bruh, I wish Thursday was legit tomorrow.

CAPULET: Bet. Head home, fam. Thursday it is, then.

(to LADY CAPULET)

Ayo, peep Juliet's mood before you crash out. Gas her up for the big day.

(to PARIS)

Peace out, my guy. I'm hitting the hay. Dang, it's so late it's basically early. Night, fam.

(everyone dips)

Act 3

Scene 5: Big Decisions

Setting: Juliet's bedroom, which looks like it's straight out of a trendy influencer's Insta story. There's an oversized, plush bed with more pillows than necessary, fairy lights strung across the walls.

(ROMEO sneaks in sneakily through the window with a rope)

JULIET: Are you dipping already? Chill fam, it's way too early. That bird you heard? That's the red Angry Bird, not the yellow one. It's still night, trust.

ROMEO: Nah fam, that was the yellow one, the herald of the morning. See those streaks of light? That's dawn breaking. Gotta go, or I'm gonna catch heat.

JULIET: You sure? That light's just Team Rocket blasting away or something. Stay a bit longer. Please.

ROMEO: Alright, I'll risk it for the biscuit. Let's pretend it's still night. That light must just be from your phone screen on max. I don't care if I get caught, how are you my love? Lets talk.

JULIET *(seeing the sun peek out)*: Wait, you're right, it is morning. You gotta go, like now! That bird is ruining our vibe. Hurry, before you get caught my guy.

ROMEO: Yeah, more light and more heartache.

(The NURSE enters)

NURSE: Miss.

JULIET: What's up, Nurse?

NURSE: Your moms is on her way to your room. The sun's up fam. Be smart. Heads up.

(The NURSE dips)

JULIET: So, the window brings in the day, and my life just dips out that same window.

ROMEO: Aight, peace out girl scout. One last kiss, and I'm gone.

(They kiss dramatically. ROMEO drops the ladder and descends)

JULIET *(shouting down at him)*: You just gonna leave like that, my love, my man? Yes, my husband, my day one! I need updates from you every single hour. A minute feels like a day, fr. If that's how we're counting, I'm gonna be a boomer by the time I see my Romeo again.

ROMEO *(shouting up at her)*: Goodbye my love, I blow you up with notifications. I promise.

JULIET: Do you think we're gonna see each other again, though?

ROMEO: No doubt. All this drama's gonna give us so much tea to spill later on.

JULIET: On god, I have this eerie feeling, like some bad vibe! Now you down there, you're looking like someone in a grave. Either my eyes are bugging or you looking mad pale.

ROMEO: Damn, mean but ok. You looking hella pale to me too. All this heartache's snatching our glow. Peace!

(ROMEO exits reluctantly)

JULIET: Why's luck always acting sus? Come back soon, Romeo.

(LADY CAPULET calls from offstage)

LADY CAPULET *(behind the door)*: Hey queen! You up?

JULIET: Who's that? My moms? Is she up late or just mad early? What's she doing up here fr?

(LADY CAPULET enters)

LADY CAPULET: What's the matter, Juliet?

JULIET: Mom, I'm just not feeling good.

LADY CAPULET: Still crying over Tybalt? Your tears won't bring him back. Too much sadness is just lame.

'

JULIET: But I gotta keep crying for such a big L.

LADY CAPULET: You feel the L, sure, but the dude you crying for ain't feeling nothing.

JULIET: Feeling this loss, I can't help but cry for him forever.

LADY CAPULET: Listen up, girl. You ain't just cryin' over Tybalt. You heated 'cause the dude who dusted him is still out there, chillin'.

JULIET: What dude, mom?

LADY CAPULET: That fool, Romeo.

JULIET *(talking lowkey so LADY CAPULET can't hear)*: Dude's legit not a villain.

(to LADY CAPULET)

Ayo cancel him! I'm deadass serious. But real talk, no one can make me feel this shook like he does.

LADY CAPULET: That's because he's still out there.

JULIET: Yeah, I'll feel better when Romeo's gone. I'm so torn up about Tybalt.

LADY CAPULET: We'll get our clapback, don't stress. Stop the waterworks. I'll slide into the DMs of someone in Mantua, where that banished Romeo is hanging. He'll whip up some gas, so he'll join Tybalt in the grave real quick. And then, I hope, you'll feel better.

JULIET *(lying af)*: For real, I'll never be chill with Romeo until I see him ded. My heart's all kinds of shook over my cousin. Mom, if you could find someone to get us some poison, I'd mix it up, So Romeo, once he takes it, Will be zooted for good. Ugh, I'm ded inside Hearing his name and not being able to get at him, to throw the love I had for my cousin right back at the guy who iced him!

LADY CAPULET: Find a way, and I'll hook us up with someone. But hey, I've got some tea that'll shock you..

JULIET: Good tea is so bussin' right now. Spill it.

LADY CAPULET: You have a solid dude for a dad. Hes planning a surprise to up your vibe. I didn't even see it coming.

JULIET: I'm hella confused.

LADY CAPULET: No cap, mad early Thursday, at Saint Peter's Church, that homie Paris gonna turn you into a bussin' bride.

JULIET: Ayo, on god, he ain't making me no bride there. This is straight-up sus. How' am I gonna marry this dude when he hasn't even slid into my DM's? Please, tell my dad, I ain't ready for a ring. And when I do tie the knot, swear it's gonna be with Romeo! There I said it. That's the real tea!

LADY CAPULET (*shocked*): Here comes your dad now. Tell him yourself, see if he vibes with that.

(CAPULET and the NURSE pull up)

CAPULET: When the sun dips, we get that light drizzle. But since my nephew got clapped, it's been pouring non-stop. What's good with you, girl? You a living meme? You gonna cry 24/7? You're like a whole mood, a ship, the ocean, and the storm all in one. Your peepers, I call 'em the ocean, are mad teary. Your bod's the ship, sailing in the salty waves of your own tears. The winds are your sighs, blowing up storms in your eyes. Your sighs and tears are wilding out. Chill or they'll wreck your whole vibe, sink your ship. So my wife, what's the word? Did you tell her our game plan?

LADY CAPULET: For real, I told her. But she's like 'nah, thanks but no thanks.' Ungrateful AF.

CAPULET: Hold up, wait a minute, wife. What do you mean? She's saying no? She ain't feeling grateful? Doesn't she get how lucky she is? Doesn't she see she's not even in the same league as this guy we found for her?

JULIET: I ain't vibing with what you picked for me. But I'm throwing you an A plus' for effort. Can't get hyped about something I'm hating on. But I can always give thanks for something if it's coming from a place of love.

CAPULET: What's all this? What's this jumbled talk? I hear you dropping 'thanks', then flipping to 'nah' and 'not feeling it', you spoiled brat. You ain't really grateful or showing any respect. But aight, get yourself set for Thursday. You're hitting up Saint Peter's Church to marry Paris. On god. You're killing my vibe heavy. You worthless girl! You looking all pale too!

LADY CAPULET *(to CAPULET)*: Bruh, chill! You on loud rn!

JULIET: Please, pops, I'm legit begging here, on my knees. Just hear me out for a sec.

CAPULET: Forget it, you're being so extra. I'll tell you what – either show up at church Thursday to marry Paris, or don't ever let me see your face again. No cap. Don't even try to clap back at me. I'm so close to losing it. Wife, we never thought we were blessed having just this one kid. But now I see she's one too many. We were straight-up cursed when we had her. She's got me salty, the little drama queen!

NURSE *(to CAPULET)*: My dude, you're buggin' to go off on her like that.

CAPULET: And you? You stay in your lane, you NPC.

NURSE: I ain't stepping outta line. Can't I even get a word in?

CAPULET: Oh, my days.

NURSE: Can't I even get a word in?

CAPULET: Nah boomer! Go spill tea with someone else. We ain't here for it.

LADY CAPULET *(to CAPULET)*: You're getting high-key mad.

CAPULET: I'm hella mad. It's got me trippin'. Day and night, every hour, at the grind, chilling, solo, in the squad, my main mission was finding her a husband. Now, I've found a guy thats valid AF. He passes the vibe check. He's like every girl's dream guy. But this girl, all up in her feels, crying like a little kid getting clapped in a Fortnight lobby, shouting, "I won't get hitched. Can't catch feels. I'm too young. Can I get a soft launch?" Well, if you won't tie the knot, cool, you get your pass. Chow down wherever, but you ain't crashing at my crib no more. Let that sink in. No cap, I ain't playing. Thursday's creeping up. Put your hand on your heart and hear my words. If you're my daughter, you'll walk down the aisle with my Paris. If not, you can bounce, beg, and die in the streets. On god, I ain't taking you back or lifting a finger for you. Facts. Think on that.

(CAPULET dips out angrily)

JULIET: Is no one up in the heavens watching my struggle bus? Mi madre, my day one, don't make me do this! Push this wedding back a month, or even a week. Or, if you can't hold off, at least let my wedding bed be in that tomb where Tybalt's chilling.

LADY CAPULET: Don't even talk to me, because I'm not gonna say a word. Do whatever, 'cause I'm unsubscribing to your trauma.

(LADY CAPULET bounces)

JULIET: On god! Nurse, how can we stop this? My man's out there, my marriage plans are like the last season of GOT. How will I ever fix them? Hook me up with some comfort. Hit me with some advice. Why's the universe gotta play games with someone as down bad as me? What's your take queen?

NURSE: Alright, here's the dl: Romeo got canceled. Banished. No cap, he ain't coming back. If he tries to slide back, it's gotta be on the DL. So, like, with things being sus as they are, I'm thinking you should swipe right on Count Paris. He's total husband material! Romeo's nothing compared to him. Facts. Paris got that light skinned stare. No joke, I'm thinking you'd vibe hard with Paris. It's a glow-up fr. And even if it's kinda meh, Romeo's 86'ed, so you can't have him anyway.

JULIET: You really feel that way?

NURSE: Facts.

JULIET: That's some solid advice. Slide into the house and tell my mom I've bounced. My dad is all in his feels, so I'm gonna hit up Friar Lawrence's pad to confess and get the all-clear.

NURSE: Aight, I gotchu. That's smart move.

(NURSE exits)

JULIET: Ugh, that snake! That absolute Twitter troll! Like, is it more messed up for her to want me to ghost my vows or to throw shade at my bae after hyping him up before? Bye, Felicia. No cap, I'm done spilling my tea to her. I'mma hit up Friar Lawrence to see his game plan. If all else flops, I've still got the power to yeet myself out of this drama.

(JULIET dips sad af)

Act 4: No Chill Zone

Scene 1: Plot Twists and Potions Mixes

Setting: *Friar Lawrence's mystical chamber, where plants are more than just decor — they're life hacks. The vibe? Think herbalist meets therapist.*

(FRIAR LAWRENCE and PARIS roll in)

FRIAR LAWRENCE: Thursday, my dude? That's like, super soon.

PARIS: Yeah, Capulet, my future father-in-law, is all about it. And I'm not sleeping on it.

FRIAR LAWRENCE: But bro, you don't even know what Juliet's thinking. That's a sketchy path to be on. I'm not vibing with it.

PARIS: She's all in her feels about Tybalt's death, so I haven't slid into the DMs yet. Love's not on her radar when she's mourning like this. Her dad thinks it's sus how sad she's getting. He's playing 4D chess, speeding up our marriage to dry her tears. She's been high key emo. If she had someone to chill with, she'd stop. That's the tea on why we're rushing.

FRIAR LAWRENCE *(to himself)*: I wish I didn't know why we should pump the brakes on this wedding. Oh, look, here comes Juliet.

(JULIET enters)

PARIS: Sup, my soon-to-be wifey.

JULIET: That's a huge maybe, sir.

PARIS *(air quoting)*: That "maybe" better be "facts" babe, come Thursday.

JULIET: If it happens, it happens.

FRIAR LAWRENCE: Facts.

PARIS: You here to spill some tea to the Friar?

JULIET: None of your business sir.

PARIS: I know you wanna tell him how you're feeling me.

JULIET: If I do, it's gonna hit different saying it behind your back than to your face.

PARIS: Girl, your face is all sad boi vibes from those tears.

JULIET: Those tears haven't done much. My face was already a mood before the waterworks.

PARIS: You're outing yourself talking like that.

JULIET: No cap, sir. It's just facts. And I said what I said.

PARIS: That #nofilter face is mine, and you're dissing on it.

JULIET: Maybe that's how it is, 'cause my face isn't even my own. Yo, Friar, you got time for me now, or should I slide through later?

FRIAR LAWRENCE: I got time for you now, my sister in christ.

(to PARIS)

Ayo, we gotta have some one-on-one time.

PARIS: No way I'm killing this moment! Juliet, I'll slide into your DMs bright and early Thursday.

(kissing her)

Damn! That kiss hits different. Catch you later!

(PARIS exits)

JULIET: Aight, close that door, and then come here and be emo af with me. This situation is a huge L.

FRIAR LAWRENCE: Oh, Juliet, I'm already caught up on your bad news. It's a puzzle that's got me stumped. I heard you're supposed to tie the knot with this simp on Thursday, and it's like, no postpones, no delays.

JULIET: Don't even start about this wedding, Friar, unless you're gonna drop some wisdom on how to . If your big brain can't bail me out, then peep my plan B. (she shows him a knife) Check this. God matched my heart with Romeo's. You were the one who high-fived us into marriage. And now, before you see me, who you hitched to Romeo, get hitched to someone else, I'm out. You're the smart cookie with all the life hacks. Toss me some advice for this hot mess. Or just watch. Stuck in this double trouble, I'm ready to play judge with my blade here. I'll fix this mess in a way you can't, even with all your book smarts and street smarts. Don't sleep on this – speak up. If you ain't got a plan B, I'm ready to yeet myself.

FRIAR LAWRENCE: Wait up, girl, I'm seeing a glimmer of hope here. We gotta go big or go home, 'cause this is majorly dire. If you're so set on ghosting life rather than getting hitched to Paris, maybe you're down for something that's like playing dead to dodge this cringe fest. You can basically fake a battle with death to dip out of this shame. And if you're brave enough, I got the cheat code.

JULIET: Bet, tell me to yeet myself off any high-rise, or to take a stroll in the sketchiest parts of town. Or park me in a field crawling with venomous snakes. Chain me up with some wild bears. Tuck me into a morgue, chilling with the dead and their creepy vibes. Or, like, shove me in a new grave, hiding with some random dead dude. All this stuff gives me the creeps just hearing it, but I'm down for whatever to keep it 100 for my bae.

FRIAR LAWRENCE: Aight, cool. Head back, keep it breezy, and play along like you're down for marrying Paris. Wednesday's coming up. Tomorrow night, make sure you're flying solo. No Nurse crashing in your room. (shows her a vial) When you hit the bed, snag this vial, mix it up with some drink, and down it. Then this chilly, sleep-like potion will cruise through your system, your pulse will bail, your skin will go all ice-cold, and your breathing will be like, "Nah, I'm out." Your lips and cheeks will lose their glow-up, and your peepers will shut. You'll look dead as. You won't move, stiff as a board. You'll be in this dead-for-the-'Gram state for forty-two hours, and then you'll wake up like it was just a chill nap. Come Thursday morning, when Paris rolls up to get you, you'll be playing dead. You'll get the full glam treatment, dressed to the nines, and they'll lay you out in an open casket, straight to the Capulet's family vault. Meanwhile, I'mma slide into Romeo's DMs about our master plan. He'll jet over here, and we'll camp out until you're back with the living. That night, Romeo's gonna scoop you up to Mantua. This whole scheme's about saving you from this trash sitch, as long as you don't flip-flop or get all scaredy-cat and bail on your own bold move.

JULIET: Hand over that vial. Gimme! Don't even trip about me being scared.

.

FRIAR LAWRENCE *(giving her the vial)*: Bet. Go do your thing. Stay fierce and nail this. I'll get a messenger to sprint to Mantua with my note for Romeo.

JULIET: Love's gonna pump me up, and that strength will make sure I can pull this off. Catch you later, Friar.

(They head out in different directions)

Act 4

Scene 2: Wedding Vibes

Setting: *The Capulet crib, where the wedding prep is hitting overdrive. It's like a reality show where everything's extra — the emotions, the decorations, you name it.*

(CAPULET rolls in with LADY CAPULET, the NURSE, and a squad of SERVERS)

CAPULET *(handing over a party list to the FIRST SERVER)*: Yo, slide these invites to everyone on this list, aight?

(FIRST SERVER takes the list and dips out)

CAPULET *(to SECOND SERVER)*: Bro, go scout like twenty fire cooks.

SECOND SERVER: Bet.

CAPULET: Ain't no whack chefs cooking for me. Gonna make 'em do the finger-lick test.

SECOND SERVER: Finger-lick test, sir?

CAPULET: Straight up. If a chef can't vibe with licking their own fingers, they ain't it chief.

SECOND SERVER: Oh, facts. Only hire the ones who can self-five their cookery.

CAPULET: Bounce then, get on it.

(SECOND SERVER yeets out)

CAPULET *(stressed AF)*: Bruh, we're lowkey unready for this wedding turn-up.

(to NURSE)

Did Juliet bounce to see Friar Lawrence?

NURSE: Yup, no cap.

CAPULET: Aight, maybe he'll chill her out. She's been acting all kinds of salty.

(Enter JULIET like she owns the place)

NURSE: Peep this, she's back from her confession looking all kinds of hype.

CAPULET: Ayo, Juliet! My headstrong lil' queen, where you been at?

JULIET *(Dropping a knee like it's hot)*: Hit up a spot where I got schooled on how ghosting my dad is a major no-no. Friar Lawrence was like, 'Get low and ask for the 'rents forgiveness.' So, here I am.

(She kneels) Pops, I'm legit sorry. From here on, I'm all ears to your words.

CAPULET: Words? Then fetch my boy Paris. Tell him about this, we're making this wedding pop off by sunrise tomorrow.

JULIET: I met your stan at Lawrence's hangout. Gave him the right amount of props, kept it classy and all.

CAPULET: Bet, this is what I'm talking about! Stand up, queen.

(JULIET gets up)

CAPULET: This is the real deal. I need to see this Paris dude. Go, fetch him. No cap, our whole squad in Verona owes big to Friar Lawrence for talking with you.

JULIET: Nurse, you down to hit my closet? Need to pick out some fierce fits for tomorrow.

LADY CAPULET: Chill, not 'til Thursday. We've got time to spare.

CAPULET: Nah, Nurse, roll with Juliet. We're hitting up the church for the wedding tomorrow, no delay.

(JULIET and NURSE peace out)

LADY CAPULET: But like, aren't we low on party supplies? It's getting late, fam.

CAPULET: Don't trip, I got this. Everything's gonna be lit, I swear. You, go help Juliet get her glam on. I'm pulling an all-nighter, no sleep squad. Imma play house husband for the night.

(LADY CAPULET dips out)

CAPULET *(to himself)*: Everyone bounced? Bet, I'll solo cruise over to Count Paris, hype him up for tomorrow. My heart's all kinds of happy, seeing our troubled girl bouncing back and getting hitched.

(CAPULET goes afk)

Act 4

Scene 3: Big Sleep

Setting: *Step into Juliet's room, now transformed into a sanctuary of emotional turmoil and bold decisions. It's like entering the eye of a storm, where calm meets* <u>*chaos.*</u>

JULIET: Yeah, these fits are bomb. But, Nurse, can you bounce for the night? Gotta DM the heavens, you feel? My life's like, mega troubled and lowkey sinful.

(Enter LADY CAPULET)

LADY CAPULET: Yo, J, you need an assist or something?

JULIET: Nah, we're Gucci. Picked out the drip for tomorrow. If it's chill with you, I'd like some me-time. Maybe Nurse can hang with you? Bet you're swamped with the sudden party prep.

LADY CAPULET: Aight, bet. Hit the hay, get that beauty sleep. You need it.

(LADY CAPULET and NURSE leave the chat)

JULIET: Peace out cruel world. Who knows when we'll link up again. Got this chilly fear cruising through my veins, like putting my life's vibe on ice. I could yell for them to come back... But nah, what's the Nurse gonna do? It's all on me. No squad. Just me. Okay, so here's the vail of poison. Kuzco's poison. What if this brew doesn't even work? Am I gonna have to say "I do" to Paris tomorrow? No way, this blade's got my back.

(She sets the knife down)

But wait, what if Friar Lawrence is on some sketchy vibes and this potion is legit poison? What if he's shook about getting cancelled for marrying me off to Romeo and then to Paris? Big yikes. But nah, he's a holy dude, shouldn't be playing me like that.
Now, what if I wake up in that tomb before Romeo slides in for the rescue? That's straight-up horror movie stuff. Will I just breath my last breath in there? No fresh air, RIP me. And if I don't peace out, I'll be chilling with the the dead in there. Old bones from way back, and Tybalt's fresh grave. That's so sus. They say spooky stuff goes down in tombs at night. Bruh, I can't even. The stench, the creepy cries, enough to make anyone lose it.

(JULIET gets real with herself)

If I wake up early in that crypt, won't I totally lose it with all that creepy stuff around me? Like, playing with my ancestors' skulls, and yanking Tybalt's body out of its shroud? What if I snap and use one of their bones to go ham on myself? Yo, I'm bugging out. Hold up, I swear I'm seeing Tybalt's ghost hunting for Romeo, 'cause Romeo iced him. Chill, Tybalt, chill! Romeo, Romeo, Romeo! This one's for you.

(She raises the vial like it's a toast)

Downing this for you, my guy.

(She sips the potion all dramatic and collapses onto her bed

Act 4

Scene 4: Overcooked

Setting: *The Capulet crib, servants are zooming around like they're vying for gold in a speed-walking competition, serving up major backstage vibes.*

LADY CAPULET: Nurse, grab these keys and cop some more spices.

NURSE: They're asking for a bunch of random ish in the pastry lab.

(CAPULET busts in)

CAPULET: Let's get this bread, fam! Party isn't gonna throw itself. Go ham on the food. Don't stress the price tag.

NURSE: Aight, housewife mode on. But you, hit the sheets. You're gonna be wrecked tomorrow staying up all night.

CAPULET: Nah, I'm good, I'm hype rn.

LADY CAPULET: Yeah, you were quite the player back in the day. But I'm cutting your party short tonight boomer.

(LADY CAPULET and NURSE head out)

CAPULET *(mumbling)*: Jealous much?

(Enter three or four SERVINGMEN with kitchen gear)

CAPULET: Ayo, squad, what's in the haul?

FIRST SERVINGMAN: Got some stuff for the chef, but no clue what it is, sir.

CAPULET: Speed it up, let's go!

(FIRST SERVINGMAN bounces)

CAPULET *(to SECOND SERVINGMAN)*: Bro, find some drier logs. Holler at Peter, he'll show you the spot.

SECOND SERVINGMAN: I got this, no need to bother Peter.

(SECOND SERVINGMAN dips)

CAPULET: That's what's up. Whoa, it's getting light out. Paris will be here soon, said he'd bring tunes. I can hear him coming.

(Offstage, music starts vibing)

CAPULET: Nurse! Ayo!

(NURSE rolls back in)

CAPULET: Wake up Juliet, get her glammed up. I'm gonna chat with Paris. Hustle, hustle! The groom's already here. Move it, I said!

(They all head out)

Act 4

Scene 5: L News

Setting: *Juliet's bedroom, once a vibe of teenage dreams and late-night chats, flips to a tragic scene straight out of a Netflix drama.*

NURSE: Miss! Juliet! Bet she's snoozing hard. Hey, lil' lamb! Hey, lady! Yo, sleepyhead! Hey, bae! Yo, madam! Sweetie! Yo, bride-to-be! What's good, you not gonna say anything? Taking that beauty nap, huh? Get all the Z's you can now. Paris ain't gonna let you chill tomorrow night, for real. She's KO'd! Gotta wake her up. Madam, madam, madam! Paris will be your wake-up call in bed. Bet he'll get you up. Won't he?

(She opens the bed curtains)

WTF? You're still in your clothes? But dead asleep. Gotta wake you.

(She tries to wake Juliet and realizes she's yeeted herself)

AYO TF? My girl's dead! I'm shook! Someone get me something to drink! My lord! My lady!

(LADY CAPULET zooms in)

LADY CAPULET: Why's it so loud in here?

NURSE: I got major L news!

LADY CAPULET: What's going down?

NURSE: Peep this, peep this! Such a tragic day!

LADY CAPULET: OMG call 911 now!

(screeches)

My baby, my everything, wake up, look at me, or I'll literally die with you! Help, help!

(CAPULET strolls in)

CAPULET: Yo, whats the hold up? Bring Juliet out. Her man's here.

NURSE: It's a wrap, she's gone, she's straight up dead. Its giving worst day ever.

LADY CAPULET: No way! She's dead, she's dead, she's dead!

CAPULET *(checking Juliet out)*: Nah, this can't be. She's ice cold. Her blood's stopped, she's all stiff. Likes shes been AFK for hours.

LADY CAPULET: Huge L!

CAPULET: Man, this is brutal! I'm big sad.

(FRIAR LAWRENCE and PARIS with MUSICIANS bust in)

FRIAR LAWRENCE: Yo, is the bride set to hit the church?

CAPULET: She was set, but she's not coming back.

(to PARIS)

Bro, the night before your big day, death snagged your girl. There she is, about to #1 victory royale but death's done its thing. Bruh, this is a huge bummer. I had one kid, my ride-or-die, my main one, and now Death's all up in my business, snatching her away! Oh man, this is straight savage! Most brutal day in the history of days, fam. This day big yikes. Never seen a day this messed up. Oh, this day's got me all kinds of messed up! Juliet got played, done dirty fr!

PARIS: Death you thief, just swooped in and nabbed her. Harsh, real harsh. Death, you're canceled! Oh, my heart! My vibe is totally killed.

LADY CAPULET: This day's straight-up cursed! My one and only kiddo, snatched by Death. It's a major L.

NURSE: Big oof! Today's pain, is pure pain. Ain't never been a day this wack!

PARIS: Fam, she got played, ghosted, dissed, and straight-up taken by Death. No cap, Death's the worst. My love, my life – it's all gone now!

CAPULET: Man, she was done dirty, straight martyred. Why does Death gotta crash our wedding? My soul's dead. My child's dead. We burying not just her, but all our joys.

FRIAR LAWRENCE: Yo, chill with the drama, for real! Flipping out ain't fixing anything. Look, you guys had Juliet with a little help from above, and now she's vibing with the angels. She's got that eternal glow-up. Sure, you couldn't stop her from dipping out eventually, but now she's got that forever life on lock. You were all about her marrying some rich dude, climbing that social ladder—that was your idea of heaven. Now you're throwing a fit even though she's literally up in the clouds, maxing out in heaven? Man, you loved her so much, it's got you acting wild. But here's the tea: It's actually better to marry fresh and peace out young than to be stuck in a long, played-out marriage. So, dry those eyes, slap some rosemary on this queen, and roll her out in her flyest fit. We gotta take her to church like it's tradition. We're all lowkey sad, but for real, we should be celebrating her level up.

CAPULET: All that hype we planned for the wedding? Flip it. It's funeral vibes now. Our lit wedding tracks are now sob songs. Our feast? More like a sad snack spread at a wake. Those joy jams? More like funeral beats. And our flowers? They're just gonna be chilling on a grave now. Everything's flipped, opposite day.

FRIAR LAWRENCE: Alright, big man, you go on. And lady, you too. Paris, you're up. Squad up, everyone. Time to escort our girl to her final cloud. Seems like the skies are throwing shade for something you did back in the day. Don't make it worse by beefing with fate.

(Capulet, Lady Capulet, Paris, and Friar Lawrence dip out)

FIRST MUSICIAN: Aight, pack up the pipes, squad. Home time.

NURSE: Fam stash those pipes. It's a high key sad vibe right now.

(Nurse exits)

FIRST MUSICIAN: Yeah, things might look up though.

(Peter enters)

PETER: We need some tunes, Alexa play Despacito!

FIRST MUSICIAN: Despacito again?

PETER: 'Cause, musicians, I'm heavy in my feels rn. DJ spin that ish.

FIRST MUSICIAN: Nah, fam. That isn't the vibe.

PETER: Y'all not gonna play?

FIRST MUSICIAN: Nah, we ain't.

PETER: Big yikes, you're canceled!

FIRST MUSICIAN: You salty?

PETER: I'm about to leave you a 1 star yelp review.

FIRST MUSICIAN: We're unsubscribing to your trauma.

PETER: Then I'ma clap back with this gat, no cap. I'll get you singing for real.

FIRST MUSICIAN: This ain't it chief.

SECOND MUSICIAN: Yo, chill with the strap, Peter. You're being extra.

PETER: Oh, you ain't picking up what I'm putting down?

(Starts singing into invisible mic)

Never gonna give you up…
Never gonna let you down…

(Speaks)

Never gonna run around and what?

(Points invisible mic to FIRST MUSICIAN)

FIRST MUSICIAN: Uh, leave you?

PETER: Wrong, major L.

(Points invisible mic to SECOND MUSICIAN)

SECOND MUSICIAN: Abandon you?

PETER: How do you not know this!?

(Points invisible mic to THIRD MUSICIAN)

THIRD MUSICIAN: I got nothing chief.

PETER (shaking his head): All of you take several seats. Straight to jail do not pass go.

(Sings)

Never gonna run around and DESERT you!

(Peter dips out)

FIRST MUSICIAN: Bruh… that dude was mad annoying!

SECOND MUSICIAN: Fr Fr.

(Musicians head out)

Act 5: The Finale

Scene 1: Endgame

Setting: *Romeo's neighborhood in Mantua, but this ain't your usual block. Think of a back-alley spot where Google Maps doesn't even go.*

ROMEO: If my dreams are spitting facts, then some news is about to drop. Love's got my heart on lock, and all day I've been vibing with this weird feeling. Had this wild dream where my girl found me dead. Crazy how dream can feel so foreshadowy right? She came over, kissed me, and bam! I was like back to life and feeling like a boss. Man, just thinking about love and my girl gets me all hyped up.

(Romeo's servant Balthasar rolls in)

ROMEO: Bruh, you got any tea from Verona? What's up, Balthasar? Got a note from the Friar? How's my girl? My dad cool? And Juliet, she good? Gotta ask that twice, 'cause if she's chillin, everything's good. She's fine then, right? Nothing's out of pocket?

BALTHASAR: Well, she's kinda fine, but not in the way you think. Her body's at the Capulet's crib, like in the tomb, but shes up with the angels now, up in heaven. I saw them put her there, then I booked it here to spill the tea. My bad for this downer news, but you said it was my job, dude. Major L.

ROMEO: On God? Then I'm calling out you, stars! You know my addy. Slide me some ink and paper, and let's book an Uber. I'm heading to Verona tonight, no cap.

BALTHASAR: Dude, chill for a sec. You're looking all kinds of sus, like you're gonna do something outta pocket.

ROMEO: Nah, you got it twisted. Bounce and do what I said. Didn't you bring any letter from the Friar for me?

BALTHASAR: Nope, no DMs from him, my lord.

ROMEO: Whatever. Just go grab us a ride. I'll catch up in a sec.

(Balthasar dips out)

Alright, Juliet, we're gonna Netflix and chill in heaven tonight. Gotta figure out how. Man, when you're desperate, those wild ideas hit different. I remember this one guy, a pharmacist, lives just around the corner. Dude's wardrobe is nothing but rags, kinda looks like Mr. Bean. He's all about those herbal remedies. Looking hella broke, tired to the bone. His shop's like a weird museum – got a tortoise shell, a stuffed gator, all these bizarre fish skins. His shelves are all 'bout that creepy aesthetic – empty boxes, green jars, some old seeds. And don't even get me started on his string collection and those dusty rose petals. Peeping all this, I thought, "Yo, if a dude needs some lethal stuff"—which would straight up get you iced in Mantua—" here's a dude so down bad he'd sell it to him." Aight, this brainwave hit me before I even needed the deadly goods. But this same broke dude gotta be my hookup. If I got it right, this is his crib. It's a chill day, so the dude should be there.

(Shouts)

Ayo! My plug!

(The APOTHECARY comes out)

APOTHECARY: Yo, who's on loud like that?

ROMEO: Slide over here, fam. I can tell you're broke. Here's forty bucks. Hook me up with some lethal stuff, the kind that hits so quick, it's running it down mid.

APOTHECARY: I've got some geeked stuff, for real. But it's straight-up illegal to sell them here in Mantua, and you get the death penalty for it.

ROMEO: You're this broke and still scared of dying? Your face is all gaunt from hunger, and I can see in your eyes you're starving. It's obvious you're #strugglebus. The world ain't your friend, and neither is the law. The world doesn't make rules to make you rich. So quit being broke. Break the law, and take this guap.

(Romeo throws a ball of cash at his face)

APOTHECARY: I'm only doing this 'cause I'm broke, not 'cause I want to.

ROMEO: And I'm paying you 'cause you're broke', hurry up old man.

APOTHECARY: Mix this with any drink, and down it. Doesn't matter if you're as big as Chris Bumstead, it'll drop you instantly.

(Hands ROMEO the poison)

ROMEO: Here's your cash.

(Hands APOTHECARY the money)

Real talk, money is like a worse poison to people's souls, doing more damage in this messed-up world than these actual poisons you're not supposed to sell. I've bought your poison. You haven't sold me anything. Peace out. Get yourself some grub and bulk up a bit. I'm taking this mix, which is more like a cure than poison, to Juliet's grave. That's where I gotta use it.

(They both dip silently)

Act 5

Scene 2: Epic Fail

Setting: Friar John's pad, which is basically a monk's version of a man cave. Picture a room with stone walls, minimal decor (because monks are all about that simple life).

(Friar John rolls in)

FRIAR JOHN: Yo, my brother in christ! What's good?

(Friar Lawrence slides into the scene)

FRIAR LAWRENCE: Sup, my bald brother.

(Dapping him up)

How was Mantua? Got any updates from Romeo? Did he sent a note back for me?

FRIAR JOHN: So, here's the tea: I was tryna link up with this other friar in town to roll with me. Dude was out here helping the sick. When I caught up with him, the health officials were all like, 'Nah, you guys might have the 'vid.' They locked us up in quarantine, no cap! Couldn't hit up Mantua, so here I am.

FRIAR LAWRENCE: Bruh, you serious?

FRIAR JOHN: Yeah, fam. I couldn't send the letter. Still got it right here.

(hands over the letter)

No one was down to deliver it, all scared of catching the plague and stuff. We're in a pandemic after all.

FRIAR LAWRENCE: Big yikes! That letter wasn't just some casual 'hey, what's up?' It was packing major info. Huge L you couldn't deliver. Should not have let you cook. Yo, snag me a crowbar, will ya? Make it snappy, bring it to my crib.

FRIAR JOHN: Aight, bro, I'm on it. Gonna fetch that crowbar for you.

(Friar John dips out)

FRIAR LAWRENCE: Guess it's just me hitting up that tomb. Juliet's gonna be waking up in like three hours. She's gonna be so shook that Romeo's out of the loop. Gotta slide into Mantua's DMs again. Meanwhile, I'll keep Jules chilling at my place until her Romeo shows. Man, this is wild. She's like a living 'seen-zoned' message, stuck in dead man's DMs. What a situation!

(Friar Lawrence bounces)

anything. Peace out. Get yourself some grub and bulk up a bit. I'm taking this mix, which is more like a cure than poison, to Juliet's grave. That's where I gotta use it.

(They both dip silently)

Act 5

Scene 3: Biggest Yikes

Setting: *The ultimate scene unfolds in the Verona graveyard, which is like the OG of eerie vibes. It's got that classic spooky graveyard aesthetic - think moonlit tombstones casting long shadows, a gentle fog rolling across the ground, and an air of solemn mystery.*

(PARIS enters with his PAGE)

PARIS: Yo, hand over the torch, lil bro. Dip out and keep your distance. Kill the light so I'm lowkey. Hide under those yew trees over yonder. Keep your ears open for anyone creeping through this graveyard. If you hear something, whistle to give me the heads-up. Toss me those flowers. Just do what I say, aight?

(The PAGE snuffs out the torch and hands PARIS the flowers)

(To himself)

Standing alone in this graveyard's kinda sus, but I gotta risk it for this.

(Page yeets to the side)

(PARIS starts laying flowers at JULIET'S tomb)

Ayo, beautiful, I'm here dropping flowers on your wedding bed. Damn, your canopy's just dirt and rocks now. Gonna make it rain with my tears here every night. Or, if not, I'll just keep laying flowers and crying. Big yikes.

(The PAGE whistles)

That whistle's my cue. Someone's rollin up. Who's out here doing graveyard strolls tonight? Who's stepping on my love tribute? Someone with a torch! Gotta ghost in the shadows for a bit.

(PARIS ducks into the dark)

(ROMEO and BALTHASAR enter, armed with random burglary tools)

ROMEO: Yo, hand over that pickax and crowbar.

(grabs them from Balthasar)

Aight, check this letter. Slide it to my dad first thing in the AM.

(hands over the letter)

Toss me the torch.

(snags the torch)

Listen, on god you gotta promise not to barge in on what I'm about to do. No matter what you hear or see, stay out of it, for real. I'm about to drop into this tomb, not just to see my girl one last time, but I gotta snag that ring off her finger. Got big plans for it. So, bounce and don't get nosy. You come back snooping, I swear I'll go beast mode and scatter your bits for the graveyard critters. I'm on a whole new level of wild right now, like, more savage than 21 savage.

BALTHASAR: I got you fam. I'll leave you to it.

ROMEO: That's a solid bro. Here's some cash for your troubles.

(hands over money)

Stay up and thrive king. Catch you later, my guy.

BALTHASAR *(Whispering but PARIS overhears)*: Even though I said I'd dip, I'm gonna chill here. Dudes got a wild look in his eyes, and I'm not vibing with his plans.

(Balthasar yeets to the side and crashes out)

ROMEO *(Speaking to the tomb)*: You death trap! You chowed down on the most precious person ever. Now I'm gonna pry open your teefs and feed you another body.

(ROMEO starts working on opening the tomb with his tools)

PARIS *(Whispering so ROMEO can't hear)*: That's that cocky kid, the dude who got the boot. He offed my girl's cousin, Tybalt. They say she died from the heartache. This guy's here to do some messed-up stuff to the dead. I'mma catch him!

PARIS *(To ROMEO)*: Ayo, hold up, you sussy baka! You're being hella sus rn, you tryna mess with the dead? You're toast.

ROMEO: Yeah, that's the plan. Came here to end it all. So chill young blood. Don't step on a guy who's lost it. Bounce, yeet, leave this place. I listened to emo music all night, let that spook you. Seriously, don't push me. I ain't tryna catch another case. Just dip, alright? Real talk, Came here to clap myself. Slide out, bro. Live. And later, you can say some crazy dude let you live.

PARIS: Nah, fam. I'm cuffing you for being sus.

ROMEO: You wanna scrap? Bet, I got nothing to lose. Let's do this!

(ROMEO and PARIS start blasting)

PAGE: Oh snap, they're throwing down! I gotta get help!

(The PAGE runs off)

(PARIS takes an arrow to the knee and collapses)

PARIS *(about to die no respawn)***:** Goddam, clapped by a 16 year old!

(PARIS dies dramatically)

ROMEO *(looking at PARIS's body)***:** Big yikes! Who is this? Oh, it's Mercutio's boy, Paris. What was Balthasar saying? I was too stressed to listen properly. Something about Paris gonna marry Juliet? Was that it? Or am I tripping? Did I just hear "Juliet" and freak out? Here, man, let me help you. We're both unlucky. I'll lay you to rest in style.

(ROMEO opens the tomb and sees JULIET inside)

A grave? Nah, this has got to be a meme, dead Paris. Juliet's here, and she's still vibing, even in death. Death, make room. You're about to get company from another lost soul.

(He places PARIS's body in the tomb)

(ROMEO, looks at JULIET, super in his feels)

ROMEO: Dudes often feel all chill right before they dip out. They say it's like the calm before the storm. But how can I even front that this is chill? Yo, my girl, my ride or die! Death's been sippin' on your breath, stealing that honey, but hasn't wrecked your glow-up. You're still fire. Your lips and cheeks still got that pop of color. Death hasn't ghosted you yet. Tybalt, you chilling over there? Bet, what's a better flex than to clap back at the same dude who got you, with the same hand, no less. My bad, cuz! And Jules, why you still lookin' so snatched? Is it like death's crushing on you, keeping you here as his boo? Not down with that. So, I'mma park it right here with you. This tomb's gonna be my crib, with these worms as our roomies. I'mma chill here for the long haul. Gonna yeet myself from all this drama. Eyes, take one last look! Arms, get in that final hug! And lips, you're the exit for my breath. Let's seal this deal with death with a kiss.

(kisses Juliet, grabs the poison)

This purple drank. You're the captain now, let's send this ship smashing into the rocks! Cheers to our downfall!

(Romeo chugs the poison)

For real, that pharmacist wasn't capping. His stuff hits fast. I should leave him a good yelp review. So this is it, going out with a kiss.

(Romeo dramatic af dies)

(Friar Lawrence stumbles in with a lantern, crowbar, and shovel)

FRIAR LAWRENCE: Baby Jesus got me tripping over gravestones left and right! Who's lurking?

BALTHASAR: Chill, it's just a homie who knows you.

FRIAR LAWRENCE: Whats good fam? What's that light over there? Looks like a new graphics card in a pre-built. Seems like it's coming from the Capulet's crypt.

BALTHASAR: Yeah, that's the spot, father. My main dude is in there, the one you're tight with.

FRIAR LAWRENCE: Who's in there?

BALTHASAR: Romeo, bruh.

FRIAR LAWRENCE: He's been there how long?

BALTHASAR: Like half an hour or so.

FRIAR LAWRENCE: Roll with me to the tomb?

BALTHASAR: Nah, can't do, Romeo would flip if he knew I was still here. Dude was dead serious about me not snooping.

FRIAR LAWRENCE: Aight, stay here. I'll check it solo. Getting major bad vibes. I'm mad worried that something's gone sideways.

BALTHASAR: So, I was catching Z's under this yew tree, right? Had this wild dream that my boss and some other dude were throwing down and Romeo clapped him.

FRIAR LAWRENCE *(approaching the tomb)*: Romeo, bro, WTF? Why's there blood at the entrance? And these blickies laying around.

(peeks in the tomb and sees Romeo and Paris)

Oh you mad dumb Romeo. And who's this? Paris, too? Looking like a crime scene? Ayo, when did this nightmare go down? Omg, Juliets still alive.

(Juliet wakes up)

JULIET: Top G! Where's my mans at? I know where I'm supposed to be, and here I am. But where's my Romeo?

(Noise comes from outside the tomb)

FRIAR LAWRENCE: I hear something. Yo, Juliet, we gotta bounce from this tomb. Looks like fate's playing us dirty. Your Romeo's out, and Paris too. Let's get you to a sisterhood or something. No time for Q&A. Security's rolling up. We gotta dip, Juliet. Can't stick around.

JULIET (in shock): Nah, I'm good. You go. I'm staying put.

(Friar Lawrence dips out)

What's this? A cup in my boo's hand? Looks like poison was his way out. Dude, seriously? You chugged it all and didn't save any for me? Guess I'll just kiss your lips. Maybe there's still some poison left for me.

(kisses Romeo)

Ayo, his lips are still warm.

(Watchmen and Paris's Page roll up.)

What's that noise? Gotta make moves. Oh snap, a knife!

(sings)

"Cause tonight will be the night that I will fall for yew"

(Juliet stabs herself with Romeo's dagger, dramatic af and yeets out)

CHIEF WATCHMAN: This is the spot, where the torch is lit. Goddam, it's a bloodbath out here. Yo, search the graveyard. Some of you, grab anyone you find.

(Other Watchmen scatter)

This is tragic. Count Paris is gone, Juliet's bleeding out. Her body's still warm, looks like she just passed, even though she's been 'buried' for two days. Someone hit up the Prince, get the Capulets, wake the Montagues. The rest of you, keep looking.
Other Watchmen head out in different directions.

CHIEF WATCHMAN: Looks like we've found the source of all this mess. But we gotta dig deeper to get the full scoop.

(Second Watchman rolls in with Balthasar)

SECOND WATCHMAN: Caught this guy, Romeo's dude, hanging around the churchyard.

CHIEF WATCHMAN: Lock him up till the Prince shows.

(Third Watchman enters with Friar Lawrence)

THIRD WATCHMAN: Found this friar all shooketh looking mad sus. Snagged a pickax and shovel off him near the graveyard.

CHIEF WATCHMAN: Sketchy. Hold onto the friar, too.

(The Prince enters with his squad)

PRINCE: What's got everyone up and wilding so early?

(Capulet and Lady Capulet make their entrance.)

CAPULET: Why's everyone losing it?

LADY CAPULET: People are out in the streets yelling "Romeo," "Juliet," and "Paris," all heading toward our family's tomb like it's a flash mob.

PRINCE: What's this major drama everyone's freaking out about?

CHIEF WATCHMAN: Bruh, it's wild. Count Paris is RIP. Romeo too. And Juliet - she was dead, but now she's like, dead again.

PRINCE: WTF? Figure out how this mess went down, ASAP.

CHIEF WATCHMAN: Here's the friar and Romeo's dude. Found them with tools, like they were busting into these tombs.

(Capulet steps up, distraught)

CAPULET: Omg peep this. Our daughter's bleeding out! That blade should be in that Montague's back, not jammed in our girl's chest.

(Lady Capulet is in shock)

(MONTAGUE enters)

PRINCE: Montague, you're up with the sun to see your son set too soon.

MONTAGUE: Prince, my wife just passed tonight. Grief over our son being banished killed her vibe. What more can this old heart take?

PRINCE: Look over there, and you'll get it.

(MONTAGUE sees Romeo's body)

MONTAGUE: Oh, my wild boy! Where's the respect? It ain't right for a son to beat his dad to the grave.

PRINCE: Ayo, chill and hold off on the clapbacks, till we sort this out. We gotta find out what popped off and get the real deets. And then I'm gonna go Judge Judy on everyone. But for now, just hang tight, be patient. Bring out the sus homies

FRIAR LAWRENCE: Look, I'm not the opp here, but I'm mad sus 'cause I was here when it all went down. So, here I am, grill me, throw shade, I've already called myself out.

PRINCE: Spill the tea, Friar.

FRIAR LAWRENCE: Imma keep it 100 'cause I ain't got time for a long story. Romeo, simplord 3000, he was Juliet's bae. And she, over there, was wifed up to Romeo. I hooked them up; they got lowkey married the day Tybalt got yeeted. That mess got Romeo canceled. Juliet was emo AF about Romeo dipping out. To fix her vibe, you all set her up with Paris. Then she hit me up, big yikes, asking for some way out of this second wedding. She was like 'I'll yeet myself in your crib if you don't help.' So I whipped up a sleep juice with my skills. It slapped. She looked dead to everyone. So like, I hit up Romeo to come through to help Juliet out of her fake grave when the sleep juice wore off. But my boy Friar John got stuck, no cap. He bounced back with my note just last night. So I yeeted over here myself, right when Juliet was supposed to wake up. I wanted to hide her in my crib till I could link with Romeo. But by the time I rolled up, Paris and Romeo were already ded. Juliet woke up and I was like, 'Yo, let's dip from this tomb, I'm shook.' But some noise had me scatter, and I dipped outta the tomb mad quick. Juliet was mad desperate and didn't roll with me. Looks like she yeeted herself. Thats the tea. And her Nurse was in on their situationship too. If I messed up, cancel me with the worst punishment.

PRINCE: That's way outta pocket. Where's Romeo's homie? What's his side of the story?

BALTAZAR: I was Romeo's main man. I slid him the news 'bout Juliet being 6 ft under, then he zoomed from exile to this tomb.

(shows a letter)

He hit me up this AM to pass this note to his pops. When he hit the tomb where Juliet was, he told me to dip.

PRINCE: Slide me that letter. I'mma peep it.

(he grabs the letter from BALTHASAR)

Where's the count's page, the one who hit up the cops? Yo, kid, what was your boss doing here?

PAGE: He pulled up with some flowers to drop on his girl's grave. Told me to back off and let him be, so I did. Then some dude with a torch rolled up to pop the tomb open. My boss got all up in his face, and that's when I yeeted out to call the squad.

PRINCE *(skimming the letter)*: This note's backing up the friar's story. It's all about their love story and the news of her RIP. Dude writes here he copped some poison from a broke pharmacist and brought it here to yeet himself and chill with Juliet. Where them haters at? Capulet! Montague! Y'all see the wack stuff that comes from your beef? Heaven's got a way of ending your happiness with love. 'Cause I turned a blind eye to your drama, I lost my peeps too. Everybody's taking an L.

CAPULET: Ayo, Montague, dap me up. That's my girl's dowry right there. Ain't asking for nothing else.

MONTAGUE: But fam, I can do you one better. Imma put up a statue of Juliet in solid gold. As long as folks call this place Verona, ain't no one gonna get more props than true and faithful Juliet. On God.

CAPULET: Bruh, I'mma make a statue for Romeo too, right next to my girl Juliet. It's gonna be lit. They were just caught up in our beef.

PRINCE: We're waking up to some real dark vibes this morning. The sun's too shook to even show up. It's giving romance tragedy vibes. Ain't no tale more full of pain than Romeo and Juliet's.

(EVERYONE FINALLY dips)

FIN

ABOUT THE AUTHOR

Chilliam Shakespeare

Meet Chilliam Shakespeare, the modern-day bard with a knack for blending classic literature with Zoomer lingo. When he's not revamping centuries-old plays, you'll find him chillin' with his squad, sipping on the trendiest caffeine fixes, and turning every situation into a meme-worthy moment.

Born into the era of digital domination, Chilliam has dedicated his craft to infusing iconic Shakespearean drama with a fresh, Gen Z twist. Armed with a pen and his ever-present smartphone, he's on a mission to prove that even the most revered classics can get a modern makeover and still slap.

Chilliam is a connoisseur of all things pop culture and a self-proclaimed "literary remix artist." He spends his days exploring the depths of contemporary slang, hunting for the perfect reaction GIF, and passionately arguing that "yeet" is a profound expression of our time.

In his downtime, Chilliam haunts local coffee houses, engaging in spirited debates about whether Romeo was the OG simp, and theorizing about the inevitable return of Elizabethan ruffs. His ultimate goal? To translate Shakespeare's entire oeuvre into a language punctuated by emojis and internet jargon, proving that words are just the start of the story.

His life's motto? "All the world's a meme, and all the men and women merely players." Chilliam believes that if Shakespeare were alive today, he'd definitely be a YouTuber with a killer Twitter account. After all, why stick to iambic pentameter when you've got viral hashtags and limitless character counts?

www.ingramcontent.com/pod-product-compliance
Lightning Source LLC
Chambersburg PA
CBHW061249170626
46809CB00007B/2908